The Replacement Fiancé

THE HOLIDAY ENGAGEMENT SERIES
BOOK ONE

LIZ DURANO

to my Lucas.

CHAPTER 1
Mariah

"Hey, Mariah! Merry Christmas!"

I look up from the paperwork in front of me to see Logan Garrison walk into the tiny office of Garrison Motors, the repair shop he and his older brother Liam both own and manage.

"Merry Christmas to you, too." I slide the paperwork back to Liam, the colorful tattoos peeking from under the collar of his t-shirt the only way I can tell the brothers apart.

"What are you still doing in town?" Logan asks, his brow furrowing.

"Having everything checked before I head up north. Fluids, air pressure, oil, tire balance... that kind of thing."

Logan studies the job estimate from over his brother's shoulder. "Pretty late for you to set out, isn't it? You're usually gone by now."

"I've got a New Year's Eve wedding to prepare for, so

I had to make sure everything was in place before I left. Suppliers, deliveries, third-party vendors, the whole shebang."

Liam's eyes narrow. "Wait! Is that the celebrity one that's all over the news? *You're* the one doing it?"

I grin. "Yup, that's me. One of the bride's friends lives nearby, and she referred me."

"That's awesome, Mariah. Congratulations!" Logan unclips sheets of paper from his clipboard and stacks them on top of a pile of receipts on the desk behind the counter, where a retro Christmas tree made of neon-green aluminum stands in the corner. I don't know why they keep putting it up every Christmas but given the other retro decorations around the office like vintage road signs and a candy vending machine that actually works, it's grown on me.

"Here you go." Liam hands me a copy of my job esti-mate. "We'll get it done as fast as we can. Could take an hour or two, maybe longer, because we're slammed."

"Don't worry. I'll put a priority tag on it. Just don't tell anyone," Logan whispers as Liam shoots him a look.

I bite my lip. "Look, guys, if there are cars ahead of me–"

"I'm kidding, Mariah. You always get priority around here," Liam says, grinning. "Anyway, is someone picking you up, or you waiting?"

"No, I'll wait. I've got some work to do anyway." I pull out my laptop. "Same Wi-Fi password?"

"Yup," Liam replies as I hand him the keys. "Triumph123."

"Thanks." I watch Liam head toward the shop where the other guys are working, whirring sounds punctuating the air as he opens the door. Of the brothers, he's the serious one, while Logan's more outgoing and friendly.

"So, you excited to be heading home?" Logan asks as he types on the keyboard.

"Kinda." Even though I don't sound too excited, I'm always happy to head back home. But that was before Mom called me a few days ago to tell me she heard my ex-fiance and his wife were going to visiting his parents next door and that they were staying until New Year's Day.

Talk about ruining the mood. It didn't even matter that we may never run into each other at all, but the fact that I could run into Elliot and Minerva during my stay was enough to send me into a panic attack, especially if they see me still single two years after they... well, ended up together.

Minerva. My former best friend's name makes me grit my teeth, but only for a second. Two years is a long time to hate someone for stealing your man, but it was always more than just the cheating. It was the years of friendship and trust that still gets me. How she could face me all that time knowing she was sleeping with my fiance I can't imagine. So, no. No way was I going to let her see me still single after two years. What if she assumed I still pined for Elliot?

Before Mom could ask me any details, I told her I had customers and would call her back. Only I never did. At least, not right away. Not until I searched online for an escort service that matched me with a man named Cooper Reed, a Nordic god with blond hair and piercing blue eyes.

Sure, he's a copy of Elliot—only more gorgeous but I didn't care. My choices simply defaulted to him because he was the only one available on such short notice. In fact, he was so new to the service that no one had snagged him yet. After a few emails back and forth and one phone call where I got to hear his deep voice, the terms were set, and the fee paid.

And just like that, I was engaged.

Now all I have to do is pick up my 'fiancé' at Sacramento Airport and during the drive to Auburn Springs, we'll iron out the details of how we met, what we like to do together and whatever things couples do together. Then we'll quietly 'split up' and go our separate ways. No one outside my family will even need to remember I was ever engaged at all.

"So, when did you get engaged?" Logan points to my left hand. "You weren't wearing that when I came by your shop yesterday."

I follow his gaze to the solitaire diamond ring gracing my ring finger. It was a last-minute purchase, something I needed to back up the surprise engagement story. At least it wasn't expensive, just a few hundred dollars, and I can have a jeweler reset it when the charade is over.

I laugh nervously. "I got engaged." As Logan's eyes widen in surprise, I add, "I... I didn't tell you?"

"I didn't even realize you were seeing anyone."

That Logan would know whether I was seeing someone is a sad state of affairs, but such has been the state of my love life for the last two years, ever since I broke off my engagement. Sure, I've tried the online dating apps but nothing has ever passed beyond the second date. There was always something going on that had to do with Always on a Tuesday Flowers, the flower shop I've owned since graduating college.

I also have to admit that at twenty-seven, I just might be enjoying being on my own a bit too much, running my own business and not getting bogged down with the nuances of being in a relationship. But that doesn't mean I've never fantasized about dating the man standing in front of me, Logan Garrison of Garrison Motors, the other half of the @GarrisonBros, as they're known online. But that's another story altogether. For now, I'm happy with the way things are with us—a friendship, nothing more. It's safer that way.

"Seriously, Mariah, what's with the ring?" Logan's voice snaps me back to the present. "How come I know nothing about this?"

I chuckle. "Just because you pick up flowers from the shop every week doesn't mean you get to know everything I do, Logan. It's called minding your own business." Gathering my purse from the counter to sit on the worn-out leather couch along the far wall, I suddenly wish they had a shuttle service that could drive me home.

But Garrison Motors is a small family-owned repair shop, and they don't have the luxury of air-conditioned reception areas or drivers who can drop me off at my apartment. And as much as taking my SUV to a service center that offered shuttle service would have been perfect right about now, I also believe in supporting small businesses just like the Garrison brothers believe in supporting my little flower shop.

I met them three years ago at a business networking event and we hit it off really well. They maintain my work vans and my SUV while I provide them with flowers for whatever occasion they need them.

"Who is this guy?" Logan's expression is serious now as he presses on, "Do I know him?"

"No."

"Where'd you meet?"

"Online."

"How?"

"One of those swipe-right things."

"When?"

"A few weeks ago."

"And he already proposed?" Logan steps from behind the counter to join me on the couch. "I mean, hell, Mariah, I can't blame him for wanting to propose to you so quickly. You're a keeper. But that was a bit too fast, don't you think? When's the wedding?"

I hold up my hand to look at the ring. Why couldn't I have waited to wear it tomorrow? Why wear it now and have nosy Logan Garrison wanting to know more about my sudden engagement?

And why do I suddenly want to tell him about it?

I let out a sigh. Whatever. Logan might as well know. After all, someone must know I'm heading to the mountains with a stranger, right? What if Cooper turns out to be a serial killer, and I end up disappearing? What the hell do I know about Cooper Reed?

"Can you keep a secret?"

Logan draws a cross over his chest. "Cross my heart."

"I hired someone to pretend to be my fiancé."

His eyes widen. "You what?"

"Just for three days, and then we conveniently break up after."

He stares at me. "You're not kidding."

"No."

"Why?" he asks.

"Because my ex-fiancé is spending the holidays next door, and I don't want him to see that I'm still single two years after we broke up."

Logan shrugs. "So what? You're over this guy, right?"

"Of course, I am!"

"So why the pretense? Not to mention the expense of hiring someone. I bet he wasn't cheap."

"No, he wasn't." I sigh again. "I know it sounds shallow, but I just didn't want people to see me still single."

"You mean you didn't want *your ex* seeing you're still single."

"It's her, actually. Minerva, the woman he ended up with."

"Why?"

"She was my best friend, and now she's his wife."

Logan winces. "Ouch. I'm sorry, Mariah."

"Yeah. Ouch is about right. Anyway, don't tell anyone, okay? It's bad enough that you know. Downright embarrassing, now that I think about it. It makes me look so... so desperate."

"Actually, it doesn't. If my girl ended up cheating on me with my best friend, you bet I'm going to show her I've moved on to someone even better. Like a total upgrade," Logan says, grinning. "And don't worry. I'm not going to tell anyone. It's our secret."

"Thanks."

"Come to think of it, you could have just asked me. I'm sure I know you better than that guy you hired." He pauses. "Where do your folks live again? Lake Tahoe?"

"Just before Lake Tahoe. It's called Auburn Springs."

His brow furrows as he thinks for a few moments. "How far is that from Nevada City?"

"Less than an hour, depending on how fast you drive. Do you know the area?"

"Chad Stoker, one of our buddies, moved up there a

year ago, and Liam and I rode our bikes up to see him back in September. Nice place," he says. "Anyway, if this guy doesn't make it, you know who to call. You don't even have to pay me a dime."

My phone rings before I can say anything. I retrieve it from inside my purse, hitting Answer the moment Cooper's name flashes on my screen. "Hi, Cooper. What's up?"

"Hey, babe, all flights from JFK are grounded until tomorrow. There's a freaking snowstorm over here," he says, his voice barely audible over the overhead announcements. "I don't think I'll make it. Definitely not in the next five hours."

"Can you get on a flight tomorrow?" Next to me, Logan doesn't budge from his spot. I know he's listening, but it's not as if I'm still keeping secrets from him. When the shop phone rings, he gets up to answer it just as two people enter the front door.

"I don't know, babe. It looks sketchy right now." As another announcement comes on, Cooper pauses, something about a list of canceled flights. He waits until the announcement finishes before continuing. "Look, Mariah, I'm so sorry. I was looking forward to meeting you in person."

"Me, too."

"I'll try to get on the first flight in the morning. Or any flight, for that matter. Right now, it's a madhouse in here. People are going crazy."

"Well, tomorrow is Christmas Eve."

He exhales. "Yeah, I know. I'm sorry, Mariah."

"It's not your fault," I say. "Do you have the address to the lodge?"

"Yeah, I do. I'll text you as soon as I get on a plane."

As I hang up and return my phone to my purse, I tell myself that it's probably for the best that Cooper can't make it. Maybe I should just wear the ring and leave it at that. I wouldn't exactly be lying if I told everyone he was stuck on the East Coast because of the snowstorm. Besides, no matter what I say, I'm sure Elliot and Minerva will think whatever they want to think anyway.

Behind the counter, Logan hangs up the phone and helps the two customers who've come in to pick up their cars. As I switch on my laptop, three more customers arrive, keeping Logan busy with repair estimates and invoicing, besides needing to go back into the shop area to help the guys.

An hour and a half later, with most of my mobile accounting settled for the day, Liam calls me over to the counter and lists down everything he and the guys completed. As he finishes ringing me up, Logan returns to the office area.

"Let me take care of that," he says as Liam steps aside. Logan waits until his brother is out of the reception area before turning to look at me. "What was your fiancé calling about? Sounded serious."

I hand him my credit card. Knowing Logan, he probably gave me a discount like he always does. "He can't make it. He's stranded in New York."

"Yeah, we have the Weather Channel playing out back, and it said something about a storm hitting the East Coast," he says, swiping the card through the terminal.

I shrug. "Maybe it just wasn't meant to be. Besides, so what if I'm still single two years later? It's not like it's permanent anyway."

"Oh, come on, Mariah," Logan scoffs. "Giving up already? Where's your fighting spirit?"

"He's stuck because of a snowstorm. I can't change that."

"I can take Cooper's place."

I stare at him. "I can't let you do that."

"Why not?" He shrugs. "It's only for a few days. We go in, act like we're together, and then head back. It's no different to how we are with each other... well, except kissing and all that."

As he slides the receipt toward me, I sign my name. "It was a stupid idea."

"No, it wasn't," he says, handing me my copy and slipping the store copy into the register slot. "I think it's a great idea, but one you can't pull off alone. You need someone... like me."

I peer at him. "You really are serious about this, aren't you? What would your girlfriend say?"

"I'm not seeing anyone right now," he replies.

"What about your Christmas plans? Aren't you spending it–"

"Liam's spending the holidays with Adriana's family

and I usually tag along. But I'm not exactly committed to it, you know? Besides, do you really want your ex and your former BFF to see you alone this Christmas?"

"Not if I can help it," I reply slowly.

"In that case..." Logan takes a deep breath. "I guess I have to do this."

"Do what?"

He clears his throat, reaching across the counter to hold my hand. "Mariah Peters, will you marry me?"

Logan

I DON'T KNOW WHAT I'M DOING BUT FILLING IN for this Cooper guy was a no-brainer. And after a night tossing and turning, I'm turning the corner toward Mariah's house to pick her up at five in the morning. With a seven hour drive ahead of us, we need this early start. Also, the sooner we get started, the less opportunity for either of us to change our minds.

To say I'm not baffled by her decision to hire some stranger to pretend to be her fiance is an understatement. *I'm right here*, I almost told her yesterday. *Right under your nose. You could have asked me.*

But that would have been... what? Too honest? Too revealing? I grip the steering wheel tighter, frustration bubbling up inside me. Why couldn't I just say it? Why is it so hard to admit that I've been harboring feelings for Mariah all this time?

Maybe because I'm afraid of ruining what we have. Our friendship, our easy banter, the comfortable routine we've fallen into over the years. It's safe. It's familiar. And now, I'm about to throw all of that into chaos for the sake of a charade.

But isn't that what I've been doing all along? Pretending to be just her friend, her reliable mechanic, when deep down I've wanted so much more?

I shake my head, trying to clear these thoughts. This isn't about me or my feelings. This is about helping Mariah. She needs me, and that should be enough. But even as I think it, I know I'm kidding myself. Part of me – a bigger part than I care to admit – is thrilled at the prospect of playing the role of Mariah's fiance, even if it's just pretend.

And that's the crux of it, isn't it? It's pretend. For a few days, I get to live out this fantasy, to be the man by Mariah's side, to hold her hand and play the devoted partner. But when it's over, where does that leave us? Can we really go back to being just friends after this?

As I pull up to Mariah's house, parking my truck in her driveway, I take a deep breath, trying to steel myself for what's to come. I'm walking a dangerous line here, and I know it. One misstep, one moment of weakness where I let my true feelings show, and everything could come crashing down.

But as Mariah steps out of her townhouse, dressed in jeans, a red sweater and a black jacket, her long blonde hair pulled back in a ponytail, I know it's too late to back out now.

For better or worse, I'm all in.

I grab the duffel bag from my passenger seat and step out. At the sound of a garage door opening, I ask, "Ready for an adventure, Mariah Peters?"

"I'm surprised you haven't backed out," she says as I slide my bag in the back compartment, next to her luggage and bags of Christmas presents.

"The Garrisons always follow through." I shut the trunk. "Come on. Let's get on the road."

"I've never done anything like this before," Mariah admits as we pull out of her driveway and head toward the main road. "I've never pretended to be engaged, let alone hire someone to pretend to be my fiance."

"You didn't hire me," I say. "I volunteered, remember?"

She smiles. "So you did. You're a good friend, Logan."

"I try." As I reach for the radio, a familiar voice comes on, singing a holiday song. "And I know you didn't ask for this, but I brought you a playlist of holiday songs just in case."

Mariah grins. "That's really thoughtful."

As we head toward the freeway, the sky is a deep purple with a hint of pink and orange on the horizon, the sunrise promising to be beautiful.

As we hit the highway, Mariah puts on the playlist, the music filling the car as the scenery passes by.

"Have you heard from Cooper?" I ask as the first song plays, *Rockin' Around the Christmas Tree*, an old favorite.

"Actually, no," she replies, frowning. "I texted him last night, but never got a reply so I tried calling him but my calls went straight to voicemail."

"He turned his phone off?"

Mariah shakes her head. "Or he ran out of charge or something. I did check the status of the flights from New York and they're still canceled. This storm is pretty bad. Runways and taxiways covered in snow, that kind of thing."

"He could have at least texted you," I say. "You paid for his service."

"I know, but there are things you just can't control," she says, shrugging. "But what's done is done. I only wanted to show Elliot and Minerva that I moved on."

"But you're not with Cooper."

"I'm with you," she says, smiling as the first song ends and the next one starts, Burl Ives singing *Holly Jolly Christmas*. "And I want thank you for agreeing to do this. Just in case he doesn't show up."

"And if he does?"

"You're a friend tagging along," Mariah says. "Until then, I guess we should talk about our engagement story. When did we meet, where did we go on our first date, and so on."

"Right. What if we met when I came to pick up flowers for a party?"

She thinks for a moment. "Why not just stick to the truth? That we met at one of those networking meetings and hit it off. Well, eventually."

"What if they ask you why they've never heard of me?"

Mariah shrugs. "We can tell them that we prefer things to be private. After all, you do have a social media presence and we could say it wouldn' t be good for your image."

I try to recall if Liam and I ever had any of the women appear on our episodes, but other than his long-time girlfriend Adriana, there haven't been. "No, they won't find anything," I finally say.

For the next few hours, Mariah asks me questions, like where Liam and I are originally from (Mount Baldy, a small mountain community east of Los Angeles) to what we like to restore and feature on our YouTube channel (vintage motorcycles), or where we went on our last road trip (Monterey Bay where we took our Triumph motorcycles on a secret route through an Army base). We figure these are a few things that she, as my girl-friend and now fiancee, should probably be aware of.

"I guess this means I'll have to watch your videos," she says as we pull up to a rest area. "I don't know the first thing about motorcycles."

"I can teach you. You'll be riding on the back of mine before you know it," I tease as we exit the car.

"Not on your life, Garrison," she replies, laughing.

"How'd a small-town Northern California girl like

you find your way to crazy LA anyway?" I ask. "Did you attend college out here?"

Mariah nods. "I attended UC Santa Barbara and worked in hotel management for three years. While visiting friends in LA I saw this listing for a flower shop for sale and I figured it was time for me to have a change of career. Besides, I love floral arranging so why not? And I've been doing it ever since."

"And you do it very well," I say, remembering the latest floral arrangement I picked up the day before. "Liam and I appreciate that you still personally do our mother's flowers."

I can almost sense her blushing. "I love them doing them for you and Liam," she says.

As we go to the restrooms, I think about how much fun it is being with Mariah, even though this is just pretend. And while I'm not an actor by any means, I find myself getting into the story as we discuss it, imagining us on a romantic stroll through downtown Auburn Springs, her arm looped through mine.

"Your turn," I say when we return to the SUV. "I need to know something about your family if we're supposed to be engaged."

"My parents own a lodge in Auburn Springs," Mariah begins as she buckles up. "It's popular with skiers on their way to Lake Tahoe but also for hosting yoga and meditation retreats. In the summer, my brother leads nature workshops. Oh, and my mom's into all the woo-woo stuff while my dad's the no-nonsense businessman.

He knows how to keep things running--balance sheets, accounting, and all that while she stocks the gift shop and runs some of the classes."

"What exactly is this woo-woo thing?"

"Don't laugh but my mother's into energy, crystals, bodywork and all that," she replies. "She'll probably assess your aura the moment you walk into the house to determine if you're a good person or not."

I grimace. "I hope I pass."

Mariah laughs. "I don't doubt it. You've got a good heart."

"Do you believe in that stuff?"

She thinks for a few moments. "I'm not sure. But I think I do."

"What about your dad? What else do I need to know about him other than he's a no-nonsense business-minded guy?"

"Dad's more practical, levelheaded which makes him and Mom a perfect pair, I guess," she replies. "He loves old trucks. In fact, he's restoring one although I can't remember what model it is."

"Any brothers and sisters I need to know about?"

"Two sisters and one brother," Mariah replies. "Emily's the oldest and she's married to a college professor, Brad, and they have one kid, Jonathan, who should be two now. They live in Colorado. Then there's Forrest, who manages the place. He lives on the property with his companion dog, Bodhi. And then there's the youngest sister, Harper. She's a fashion and lifestyle vlogger. She'll probably film everything, so be forewarned."

"So they'll all be there?"

Mariah nods. "They can't wait to meet you."

I stare at the road ahead, my mind racing with the things I need to know about Mariah and her family, as well as our engagement story. But the more we talk, the more natural it all feels, almost like we really are dating, and the thought makes me smile.

"What are you thinking about?" she asks.

"Nothing," I reply as the sun shines brightly over us. "Just enjoying the ride."

"Oh, come on!" Mariah presses on. "I know that look. What's on your mind?"

"Just thinking about what I know about you."

What do you know about me?" she asks, her tone playful.

I clear my throat. "For starters, you like flowers or you wouldn't be a florist." At this Mariah rolls her eyes but I press on. "You like wearing dresses with flowing sari skirts--which I like, by the way. You pick the perfect colors that compliment your skin and your hair." I almost say the compliment her eyes and her smile, but I remind myself to keep things platonic. "And you're really funny. That's something I didn't expect."

"Thanks," she says. "What else?"

"You enjoy reading. Real books, not those digital e-readers," I continue as Mariah looks on with surprise. "You borrow them from the library and I know this because you leave them on the counter sometimes and I see the library catalog numbers on the spines. And you like patchouli."

She looks at me incredulously. "Patchouli?"

"I smell it on your whenever you hand me the flowers every week," I say. "I'm not saying it's bad or anything but I like how it's subtle and mixed with something else."

"Honeysuckle," she replies, bringing her wrist to her nose. "My mother makes it and it's one of my favorites."

I grin. "It's one of my favorites, too. It suits you." I pause, clearing my throat. "Anyway, that's all I know about you."

Mariah laughs. "That's more than Cooper will ever know about me." Suddenly her eyes widen and she glances at her phone. "What if he's at the airport right now?"

"Who? Cooper?" I ask. "Did he just text you?"

She shakes her head. "His original flight is supposed to arrive in an hour. Do you think we can stop by the airport and see if he made it?"

A stab of jealousy rushes through me. I shake my head. "Are you serious? You're thinking about seeing if this guy made it? After all the trouble you went through to hire him? Come on, Mariah."

"What if his phone battery died and he made it on a flight after all?" she asks. "I just want to make sure, that's all."

"And what if he did make it? What then? Are you showing up with two fiances?"

"I'd hate having him arrive without me there to pick him up. But for all we know, his flight got canceled after all and he's still in New York, but..." Mariah pauses and I can tell the uncertainty on her face. "Can we stop by the airport anyway for my peace of mind?"

I sigh. "Okay. Let's do it."

CHAPTER 3

Mariah

THE AIRPORT IS TEEMING WITH PEOPLE WHEN we arrive. With Logan refusing to drop me off at the Arrivals terminal in case we lose each other, we find parking and make our way to the terminal together.

I don't even know what to do if Cooper shows up. Somehow, I didn't think this plan through, but if Cooper shows up, he'll have to pretend to be a friend tagging along. After all, it's Christmas Eve, and I can't turn him away just because I found a replacement.

Logan takes my hand and holds it the whole time. His hand dwarfs mine, rough in places but warm. It brings visions of us snuggled under a blanket in front of the fire, but I push the thought away. I need to focus on finding Cooper in the crowd.

As we stand in front of the double doors of the Arrivals gate, we look like a normal couple expecting a friend to arrive.

"His flight just got in," he says as we look at the board with its flight names and times. "What does he look like?"

I pull out my phone and scroll through my messages. Cooper still hasn't called or texted, and I'm worried about him. *Is he okay? Why hasn't he replied to my messages?*

I pull up his photograph and hand the phone to Logan. It's a picture of a man wearing a nice suit leaning against a Ferrari. With his blonde hair, blue eyes, and dazzling smile, he's like the 21st-century version of Paul Newman.

Logan frowns. "You hired some actor?"

"No, not an actor. He's an escort."

Logan glances at me quizzically. "You do know that escorts don't just pretend to be a fiancé or boyfriend, right?"

"Our contract does not include any sex," I say, knowing I sound so naïve. "I told him all I wanted was for him to pretend to be my fiancé."

"I hear those other things are not usually in the contract," he says. "It's mostly an understanding."

"How would you know that?"

Logan shrugs. "I've seen the movies."

"I didn't have any plans beyond holding hands with him. Honest." I pause. "Maybe a kiss under the mistletoe, if necessary, but beyond that, it was just him pretending to be my fiancé and we went our separate ways."

Logan doesn't speak for a few moments. "You seriously had a contract?"

"The agency had its own contract, but I had to draft one for my special request," I say. "There were certain... duties as far as his job description. Besides, I figured my parents would put us in separate rooms anyway, so there was no risk of anything else happening. And I wanted nothing to happen other than what had been outlined..." I pause, realizing how defensive I sound. But no matter how I word it, the facts are the same: I hired an escort.

"What exactly did you outline? What could he do and not do?"

I clear my throat. "Well, holding hands is okay."

"And?"

"Maybe a kiss. Not a deep one. Just a simple kiss."

"No tongue?"

I glare at him. "Of course not."

"That's it?"

I nod. "Yup. That's pretty much it. It's just for the holiday weekend. I mean, I have a wedding to take care of right after Christmas."

I can almost see relief on Logan's face as he hands me back my phone. "You've got me curious about this contract now."

"Don't be. It was more like a grocery list. With bullet points."

"That sounds romantic."

I chuckle. "It was... for, like, two seconds." It was

also last minute. It didn't even matter if he looked like Paul Newman or if this was his first job since joining the agency. I just needed him to pretend to be my fiancé for a few days.

We wait a few more minutes, scanning the oncoming crowd of passengers walking out of the Arrival gate but seeing no one who matches Cooper's description. When the crowd thins thirty minutes later, Logan asks one of the passengers if he's from one of the canceled flights from yesterday, and the man says yes, and that others ended up getting on different planes with out-of-the-way connecting flights.

"But that's Christmas Eve for ya," the man says just as we spot the crew exiting the terminal. As the realization hits me that Cooper isn't on the flight, I'm ashamed to feel both disappointment and relief.

"Let's check to see when the next one comes in." Logan takes my hand, and we make our way to the board but find no other flight coming in from New York within the next two hours. We spend the next twenty minutes checking online schedules on our phones to find connecting flights headed for Sacramento. Maybe he took one of those. But the longer we search, the more hopeless it seems to figure out which flight he could be on—if he's even on a flight. The news back east still said that only a handful of flights got out, and those were all full.

"What do you think we should do?" I ask as I look

up from my phone. "Until he texts me back, it'll be like looking for a needle in the haystack."

"It's up to you, but the longer we stay here, the later you'll get to your parents' place. And if I remember correctly, there's a winter storm in effect tonight," he says. "They could end up closing the roads up the mountain."

I glance at my phone again, wishing Cooper would have texted me back, but Logan's right. We need to hit the road.

"Let's go then."

Logan takes my hand again, and we make our way through the crowd of people back to the SUV. He lets go only when we get to the SUV and pulls open the passenger door. "Hope you don't mind me holding your hand like that, but if I'm supposed to be your fiancé, I should start acting like one. It is on your grocery list, right?"

"Yup, with pizza being your favorite food of all time."

"With pepperoni and sausage," he adds. "No pineapple."

"I'll make sure to let my vegan family know about it."

Logan's jaw drops, and he stares at me in horror. "I sure hope you're not serious because I'm not settling for turducken tonight. We'll have to do some serious shopping before we hit the road."

I laugh. "I was just kidding."

He lets out a long sigh of relief. "For a minute, I thought you were serious."

I chuckle. "Don't worry, Logan. Even with all the patchouli you're about to inhale back there, we're a meat-eating family."

We make it back on the road, and this time, we keep conversation to a minimum. It allows me to settle into the vibe of home that I've missed so much, one that I sometimes wonder is still for me. If I were to leave everything behind in LAand come back here, would I be happy? I don't know the answer to that, just as I don't know if I'll ever find a man just for me.

Is it because I'm too busy with work to give any man my time? It's not like I haven't been out on dates since Elliot and I broke up. Two years is a long time to pine for someone, and I certainly didn't. But maybe I've been guarding my heart more than I should.

Is that why I haven't met anyone who can make my heart beat faster or the butterflies in my belly flutter? Well, except for Logan earlier in the morning when he talked about the pink and red skirts I wore to the shop. But I remind myself that Logan's just observant.

"We need to get our stories straight, Mariah," he says, breaking the silence in the cab. "How long have we been seeing each other?"

"Six months."

"When did I propose?"

"Um, two weeks ago."

"Where did I propose?"

I bite my lip. "I haven't thought about that."

"Well, if I proposed to someone, I'd do it where we had our first date."

"That reminds me, where did we have our first date?" I ask.

"I'd have taken you for a ride on my motorcycle up to Newcomb's Ranch," he says. "It's twenty minutes on the Angeles Crest Highway, and one of LA's best-kept secrets... unless you're a biker then it's not. Then we'd stop at the Roadhouse for a bite to eat."

"Where else have we gone?"

He thinks for a moment. "What about the Santa Monica Pier? Have you been on the Ferris wheel?"

"No, not yet."

"Let's say that the first time I kissed you was on the Ferris wheel," he says, grinning. "What about the rest of the time when we're not out and about? What do we like to do together?"

I shrug. "Movies?"

"What's the first movie we saw together? Or the last?"

"I don't know. I haven't seen a movie in years."

"Then we can't use that. We're bound to stumble there." Logan thinks for a few moments. "What about hanging out at the beach or at home? With you and me having our own businesses, let's say we like to just chill at home."

"That should work," I say. "It's more my speed, definitely."

We don't speak for a few moments, Logan's attention on the road ahead and mine on the blur of trees outside the window. I can smell the scent of pine in the air, and feel the chill of a Christmas winter in the wind.

"What about you?" I ask. "What do I need to know about your family other than every Friday, you visit your mom at the cemetery?"

Logan doesn't answer right away, but I see his brow furrow. "Other than Liam and me being tight, not much, really."

"Your dad? Didn't he hand you the shop?"

"Not exactly. He just walked away from it one day and left everyone hanging," he says. "At first, Liam and I took over because the guys hadn't been paid, and suppliers threatened to sue the shop. We didn't know much about running a repair shop then, but we learned on the job, and because we already enjoyed tinkering with engines and all that, it wasn't too difficult a transition."

"How old were you?"

"That was ten years ago, so I was seventeen, and Liam was twenty."

"Seventeen's too young to be running a business," I say. "What about school?"

"Liam quit college to run the shop full time while I worked after school and on weekends," Logan replies. "By the time you and I met, Garrison Motors was in a better place. Everyone got paid, and suppliers were happy. Dad was long gone then, and it was all for the best. The guys who worked for him mostly stayed with us until a few retired."

He pauses, then sighs. "And that's pretty much all you need to know about me."

From the way I see Logan's Adam's apple bob up and down as he swallows, his gaze firmly on the road ahead, I know we're done talking about his family.

That's when it hits me.

He could have spent Christmas with Liam and Adriana, but Logan chose to spend it with me instead, pretending to be someone he's not.

CHAPTER 4

Logan

"Soraya," I say, testing the name on my tongue as we drive through the entrance of Soraya Lodge Bed & Breakfast, a sprawling five-acre property nestled in the Sierra Nevada Mountains comprising a main building with its cabin-style structures, three free-standing cabins and a round structure for workshops. "What does the name mean?"

"It's a Persian name my mother fell in love with when she was younger," she replies. "It means dazzling light or jewel. It also stands for the Pleiades, a cluster of nine stars in Taurus that you can see in the summer."

"Will you show it to me one day?"

She nods, a simple "Sure," but I catch the nervousness in her voice. As we near the main house, I notice her glancing at me, her anxiety palpable.

"Logan, maybe I should just tell them you're a friend, just in case—" she starts, but I cut her off gently.

"Aren't they expecting you to show up with your fiancé?" I remind her, trying to calm her nerves. When she tries to protest again, I place my hand over hers. "Everything will be fine, Mariah. We're here, and no matter what happens, we'll have a good time. Do you really want to back out now?"

I see the resolve settle in her eyes as she shakes her head. "No."

"There you go," I say, feeling a mix of relief and anticipation.

As we arrive, the sound of laughter spills out from the main house. Mariah suddenly grabs my hand as I'm about to open the car door.

"Wait! What if they ask about a wedding date?" she asks. "We haven't set one. If we were really engaged, we'd have set one by now given we're both busy with our shops."

But before we can discuss it further, the front door opens and Mariah's family pours out. As her sisters rush toward us, she whispers their names. "That's Emily with the ponytail and that's Harper with the camera."

"Oh, my! He's gorgeous," I hear Emily say, and I feel a blush creeping up my neck. "You never told us he was tall, dark, and handsome. Definitely an upgrade from–"

"Emily!" Harper cuts her off with a look before turning back to us with a smile. "Now I know why you kept your engagement a secret. I know I would. I'd hate sharing him with anyone."

I try to keep my composure as the sisters approach.

"You must be Harper and Emily. Mariah's told me so much about you," I say, accepting their hugs.

"And he gives amazing hugs, too!" Harper exclaims before dashing around the SUV towards Mariah. The door opens again and an older man with salt and pepper hair makes his way toward us.

"You two finally made it," he says, shaking my hand. "I'm Ewan Peters."

"Logan," I say. "Thank you for having us."

"My pleasure." He claps me on the shoulder. "When my wife told me Mariah was bringing her fiance for Christmas, I couldn't believe it. Our Mariah, engaged! And here you are."

I smile, trying to appear as genuine as possible. "Here I am indeed, sir."

Just then, a woman with long silver hair streaked with lavender highlights emerges from the house. Her eyes light up when she sees us, and she practically floats down the steps. This must be Mariah's mother.

"Oh, welcome, welcome!" she exclaims, enveloping Mariah in a hug before turning to me. "And you must be Logan. I'm Harmony, Mariah's mother."

As she hugs me, I catch a whiff of patchouli and lavender. When she pulls back, her eyes seem to study me intently.

"I just love your energy, Logan," she says, her voice dreamy. "It's so refreshing... so light and almost purple along your third eye."

I blink, unsure how to respond to that. Mariah had

warned me about her mother's... unique perspectives, but experiencing it firsthand is something else entirely.

"Thank you," I manage to say, hoping it's an appropriate response.

"Thank goodness for that," Emily chimes in with a laugh. "Because if he didn't have that energy, she'd watch him like a hawk guarding her young the whole time. And I'm sure Forrest will be, too."

"Where is he?" Mariah asks, and I'm grateful for the change of subject.

"He's checking on a guest who rented one of the cabins but has no clue how to use the wood stove," Mrs. Peters replies. "We can't have freezing guests now, can we?"

"Nope," Mariah says, shaking her head and giggling. I can't help but smile at her laughter. It's a sound I've always enjoyed, even before this whole engagement charade.

"But you'll see him in time for dinner," Ewan adds.

Suddenly, Mariah's voice drops to a whisper. "Are they here?" she asks, glancing towards a house in the distance. I assume she's referring to her ex and his family, though I don't dare ask for clarification.

Mrs. Peters nods. "We ran into them this morning, and they said hello."

"You never wait this late to come up," Ewan remarks as we head towards the house. "But I'm glad you made it, honey. The news of your engagement has made the holidays more exciting around here. The whole town knows."

I feel Mariah stiffen beside me, and when I glance at her, she mouths 'I'm so sorry' with a look of horror. I just shrug. What else can I do? We're in this now, for better or worse.

As we step inside, I'm hit with the warmth and the scent of pine and cinnamon. A Christmas tree stands in the corner, and beside it, a young boy is playing under the watchful eye of a man I assume is Emily's husband.

"Logan, this is Brad, Emily's husband," Mariah confirms my guess as she introduces us.

I shake Brad's hand, exchanging pleasantries. As Mariah's parents excuse themselves to finish preparing dinner, I find myself falling into an easy conversation with Brad about motorcycles. It's a welcome distraction from the nerves that have been building since we arrived.

But even as I chat with Brad, I can't help but be hyper-aware of Mariah's presence, of the weight of the role we're playing. I catch her glancing our way occasionally, a mix of emotions playing across her face that I can't quite decipher.

This is going to be an interesting few days, I think to myself. I just hope we can pull it off without anyone getting hurt – especially Mariah.

As Emily and Mariah's mom take over watching Jonathan, Brad and I fall into easy conversation. When he learns I ride a motorcycle, his eyes light up with interest.

"Really? What do you ride?" he asks eagerly.

"I've got a Triumph," I reply, unable to hide my enthusiasm. It's always nice to meet another bike enthusiast.

Brad nods appreciatively. "Nice. I've been thinking about getting one myself, though Emily's not too keen on the idea."

I glance over at Emily, catching her slightly disapproving look. I can relate—I've known plenty of partners who weren't thrilled about their significant others riding.

"They're great machines," I say, trying to strike a balance between my love for bikes and not wanting to cause marital strife. "But they do require a lot of respect and caution."

As we continue talking, the conversation shifts to different types of bikes. I find myself explaining the differences between various models, the pros and cons of each. Brad is particularly interested in Harleys, and I share what I know about them.

I'm so engrossed in our conversation that I almost don't notice Mariah approaching until I feel her hand on my shoulder.

"Hey, would you like me to give you a tour of the place before it gets dark?" she asks.

"Sure, love," I reply, covering her hand with mine and flashing her a smile. I notice a flicker of something in her eyes—nervousness? Or maybe something else? It's hard to tell, but I remind myself to stay in character.

We're engaged, after all. At least, that's what her family thinks.

As we prepare to head out, Harper hands Mariah some keys. "The shop is closed right now, so you'll need this," she says. "Make sure you write down what you bought, or Mom will go crazy wondering if she forgot to write down a sale."

We step outside, and the crisp mountain air fills my lungs. It's refreshing after being in the warm house, surrounded by curious family members.

"So, where to first?" I ask, trying to sound enthusiastic despite the lingering anxiety about our charade.

Mariah leads me towards the main lodge. "I thought we'd start with the gift shop," she says quietly. "I need to grab something, and it'll give us a moment alone to... regroup."

I nod, understanding her need for a breather. This whole situation is more intense than I'd anticipated. As we walk, I take in the beauty of the property. The snow-covered ground, the towering trees, the charming cabins – it's like something out of a postcard.

Inside the gift shop, Mariah heads straight for a display of leather bracelets. "I thought I'd get you one of these... for tomorrow morning when we open our presents," she explains, her voice low. "It'll add to our story, you know? A little gift from the local shop."

"Smart thinking," I whisper back, impressed by her quick thinking. "Which one do you think suits me best?"

She picks up a dark brown leather bracelet with a platinum clasp. "This one," she says, holding it up to my wrist. "It matches your watch."

As she fastens it around my wrist, our eyes meet, and for a moment, I forget we're pretending. Her touch is gentle, and I find myself wishing... No. I can't go there. This is just an arrangement between friends. Nothing more.

"Thanks," I say, clearing my throat. "It's perfect."

After Mariah jots down the purchase in a ledger, we continue our tour. She shows me the yoga building, the free-standing cabins, and points out her brother Forrest's cabin at the edge of the property.

"So, Forrest is the one checking on the guest who can't use the wood stove?" I ask, remembering the earlier conversation.

Mariah nods, chuckling. "Yeah, it happens more often than you'd think. City folks, you know?"

As we walk, I can sense Mariah relaxing a bit. She starts sharing stories about growing up here, about the competitions she and her siblings would have over who could make beds the fastest. It's endearing, and I find myself genuinely interested in learning more about her childhood.

We're nearing the main house again when Mariah suddenly stops. "Logan," she says, her voice serious. "I just... I want to thank you again for doing this. I know it's a lot to ask, pretending to be engaged and all."

I turn to face her, placing my hands on her shoulders. "Hey, what are friends for, right? Besides, your family seems great. I'm having a good time."

She smiles, but I can see the worry in her eyes. "Just... if it gets to be too much, let me know, okay? We can always come up with some excuse..."

"Mariah," I say firmly, "we've got this. Remember, I've known you for three years. I think I can manage to pretend to be in love with you for a few days."

The words come out before I can really think about them, and I see something flicker in Mariah's eyes. Surprise? Hope? But before I can analyze it further, the moment passes.

"Right," she says, straightening up. "We should head back. Dinner will be ready soon, and Forrest should be there by now."

As we walk back to the house, I find myself wondering about that look in Mariah's eyes. And if I'm being honest, I'm a little surprised by my own words. Pretend to be in love with Mariah? Maybe it won't be as hard as I thought.

But I push those thoughts aside as we reach the front door. We have a role to play, and I intend to play it well. Whatever happens after this weekend, well... that's a bridge we'll cross when we come to it.

CHAPTER 5

Mariah

WE TAKE A LONG WAY BACK TOWARD THE house, past the vegetable gardens, currently barren and covered with snow, and a barn Dad converted into a garage. It's where he stores the truck that he's been restoring for years. As we peer through one of the windows, even Logan gasps.

"Oh wow! That's a Fleetside," he says excitedly. "I wonder if that's a 265-cid V-8."

I laugh. "You better ask him. For a second there, I could have sworn you spoke a foreign language."

After a few minutes of peeking through the windows, I pull him away from the barn, and we return to the trail leading to the house.

"I'd love to ride up here along with my brother and the guys one day."

"Summer's a great time to do that. The lake is two miles from here. You can go swimming, fishing, or just sunbathe. There's canoeing, too, if you're into that. Or kayaking. Summer's also when the Soraya is usually busy with nature workshops."

"I'd love to come and visit one day," Logan says. "Liam and Andriana would love this."

I suddenly freeze in place, my gaze on two couples walking along the trail toward us. "Crap! It's Elliot and his parents..." I pause, my throat tightening. "And Minerva."

"Why are you whispering?" Logan asks, his voice lowering.

"Because I have no idea what to say to them."

He takes my hand, squeezing it. "A simple Merry Christmas will do fine. You've moved on, remember?"

They stop when they see us approaching, as if they, too, are debating what to do next. After a pause, three of them head back in the opposite direction, leaving only Elliot standing along the trail waiting for us. I can't believe he didn't go back with his parents and Minerva, but it's also classic Elliot. He was never one to back down from anything and certainly not from me.

With his blond hair, aquiline nose, and wearing a V-neck brown sweater over a light gray t-shirt and blue jeans, Elliot could have stepped out of a men's fashion magazine. It brings back memories of how fussy he used to be about every piece of clothing he owned. Everything had to be perfect, every suit tailored, every shoe he owned buffed to perfection. Even his dress shirts were purchased from London's Saville Row. I should have noticed how my best friend had been more in tune with his fashion tastes than I was, but I push the thoughts away as Logan squeezes my hand again, a reminder that I'm not by myself.

I'm engaged.

"Hey, Mariah," Elliot says. "Merry Christmas. You look good."

If he's fishing for compliments, he's about to be disappointed. "Merry Christmas to you, too," I mumble.

"I hope you guys are doing well," he says, his gaze going from me to Logan.

"We are." I grip Logan's hand tightly. This is it. Show time. "Anyway, I'd like to introduce you to my fiancé, Logan Garrison. Logan, this is Elliot."

Elliot stares at Logan for a few seconds before shaking his hand. "You're one of the Garrison brothers. I subscribe to your YouTube."

"That's me," Logan says, his expression serious. "It's very nice to meet you."

"Congratulations on your engagement," Elliot says, his gaze moving to me. "I'm very happy for you both."

I'm sure you are, I almost say as sarcastically as I can, but I don't. The man was always polite... until the day I caught him and Minerva together. But I force a smile before the memory ruins my holidays. "Thank you."

The silence that follows is palpable as if we've lost the ability to do any small talk.

Elliot clears his throat. "I'm sorry for using this trail

that goes through your place. If I'd known you were going to be here, we would have used the other trail."

"It's no big deal. We're all neighbors," I say cheerily as Logan turns to me.

"Ready to go, love?" he asks, looking at me with an intensity I've never seen before.

"Yup, I'm ready." I turn to Elliot. "Well, it was nice chatting with you."

With a wave goodbye, Logan and I walk past Elliot and keep going, neither of us talking until Logan urges me to slow down with a gentle tug of his hand.

"That wasn't so bad, was it?" He smiles. "You've moved on."

"Is it so bad to want to show him that I got the better part of the deal?" I ask we near a small bridge and stop.

"No, it isn't. He may have hurt you in the past, but you've shown him that you've moved on." Logan grins. "I liked the part where he actually watches our channel."

"I definitely got the better part of the deal." I pause. "Anyway, this was what I wanted to show you before we got interrupted."

"It's beautiful," Logan murmurs as I let go of his hand and lean back against the railing.

"I used to go across this bridge when I was a kid to get to the blackberries that grew just beyond the trees." I point to the crop of fir trees in the distance. "You had to deal with the thorns, but I didn't care. I'd pick as much as I could and eat them right on the spot. Mom and Dad used to find out I snuck out because I'd come home with purple fingers and lips. And scratches on my fingers."

Elliot used to go with me, too, but I don't mention that tidbit. It's the past.

This is my present.

Standing in the middle of a small bridge, we watch the creek flowing below us. I take a deep breath and close my eyes, forcing all thoughts of Elliot and Minerva away. I knew this would happen, and it wasn't as bad as I thought. But if there's one positive thing about running into Elliot again, it's that I felt nothing for him at all. There was just... nothing. The only thing I really feared was him seeing me still alone.

"Mariah, we need to talk about something before we go back into the house," Logan says as I turn to face him. "We never discussed just how this pretend thing will be, like what's on the table and what isn't. I would assume you don't want us to appear cold in front of them, right?"

"Definitely not," I reply. "That would make this whole engagement thing useless."

"When you came up with this idea and hired the other guy, what did you have in mind when he'd arrive and play his role?"

"I never really put a lot of thought into it, to be honest," I stammer. "I was so busy getting everything ready for the New Year's Eve wedding that I figured Cooper would know what to do and how to do it."

Logan doesn't speak for a few moments, his brow

furrowing as he gazes at the water below us. Then he takes a deep breath and faces me. "All right, let's try this." He takes my hand and brings it to his lips. They're warm and soft, his day-old stubble tickling my skin.

My cheeks burn with embarrassment. *Do I really need tips on how to react to a man kissing the back of my hand?*

Apparently, I do, blushing optional.

"That... that feels nice."

"And this?" His other hand moves up toward my face, his fingers warm against my cheek, his thumb brushing along my chin. It sends delicious tingles running up and down my spine.

"Um... that's nice, too."

"Don't giggle," he murmurs, his gaze serious. "He's still watching us, you know."

My eyes widen. With Elliot behind me, I can't see a thing. "He is?"

"The woman... Minerva came back. She went around the vegetable garden," he says. "They're both watching us."

"The nerve–"

"Close your eyes."

I do what Logan says and wait. I should know what's coming next. After all, I've lost count of how many times I've secretly wondered how it would feel to be kissed by Logan Garrison. I feel him move his face closer, his cologne mingling with the faint scent of leather and motor oil, making my stomach clench.

When the kiss comes, it takes my breath away. It's soft, our lips barely touching, our breaths warming the barest of space between us. It's as if time decided to stand still at that moment, making every millisecond count until our lips touch.

But they don't.

That's because my phone buzzes from inside my jacket. In my panic, I pull away, fumbling for my phone and tapping the display. *Why do I feel like I'm doing something I shouldn't be doing?*

A message from my shop manager appears on the screen.

CORA

Merry Christmas, boss! Just wanted
to let you know the day's sales
numbers have been uploaded and
everything is set up for NYE wedding.
Will be back at the shop on the 26th.
Merry Christmas!

MARIAH

Thanks for the update. Merry
Christmas to you too

"Work?" Logan murmurs as I put my phone away, the opportunity for the kiss I never realized I'd been waiting for all these years now gone.

I sigh. "Talk about timing, right?"

"It counts as practice," he says, smiling. "I just don't want you acting surprised when it happens in front of everyone."

I take a step closer, suddenly feeling bolder. "Why don't we try it again? You know, just to be sure we don't get anything wrong."

"How presumptuous of you to think we'd get it wrong." Logan chuckles as his head dips lower. "Next time, let the phone ring."

Before I can reply, his lips touch mine, and I catch my breath. Who knew it's been so long since I'd been kissed? A proper kiss, one that makes me weak in the knees while the butterflies in my belly are going crazy.

Logan's kiss starts off slowly, just the barest brush of his lips against mine, causing a stirring inside me that feels like fireworks in slow motion. Fireworks in the middle of a snowstorm.

He nips my upper lip first and then my lower lip before finally kissing me, his mouth moving against mine, and he doesn't stop until our tongues meet. He tastes like nothing I've ever experienced before, a mixture of coffee, leather, and something delicious that I want to taste over and over again.

A slow and tortuously delicious kiss that has me standing on my tiptoes so I can have more.

Logan pulls me closer, lips against lips, tongue against tongue, our bodies pressed together. My arms go around his neck, holding on for my knees are about to buckle. How can a simple practice kiss render me suddenly helpless?

But this isn't a simple kiss. This isn't even practice.

This is real.

I pull away, surprised at my thoughts and how my body responds to him. It's buzzing with electricity as if I'd just touched a live connection. But there's something else, something that goes even deeper. Why do I feel like the floodgates to emotions I've never acknowledged have finally been flung open—the giddiness, the happiness, the fear?

That I'll be alone again at the end of this charade.

"We should go back inside," I stammer. "That's enough practice for now."

"Yeah, maybe we should." His voice is almost hoarse when he speaks, the lines on his forehead more prominent now as he gazes at me. It's as if he's just as surprised as I am, although why I have no idea.

Logan is only doing me a favor, after all. He's only pretending to be someone he's not. And after this is all over, we'll go back to the way things were... as friends.

CHAPTER 6

Logan

WHOA. I DIDN'T EXPECT THAT.

Hell, I didn't expect anything. But what happened just now is rocking me to the core. I've always considered Mariah to be beautiful—inside and out—but I've always reminded myself to see her as a friend, the way one observes someone they know is out of their league. It means that their only choice is to watch them from afar and, in my case, from the other side of the counter. Hers and mine.

But that was before that kiss, one that felt like I'd just been hit by a Mack truck.

If I had thought pretending to be Mariah's fiancé would be a piece of cake, boy, was I wrong. So wrong. Now there's nothing more I want than to keep going, but at the same time, I hate that it's all pretend.

Mariah takes my hand and holds it all the way to the

front door of the Peters' home. Elliot and his wife are gone, but that doesn't matter. The charade is back on.

"You okay?" She asks as we stand in front of the door. "You're quiet all of a sudden."

I shrug. "Just thinking, that's all."

"I'll make sure to tell them to lay off you if they give you a hard time."

"Nah, it's all right. It comes with the territory."

It was also my idea to sign up for this, simply because I figured it was something that would take my mind off another Christmas without Mom. Instead, everything about Mariah's family has brought back memories of Mom and her kitschy decorations that Liam and I used to hate growing up but treasure every single one since she got sick.

I remember how her mere presence could light up any room, like the way Mariah's smile does. But whether Mariah's family has only made my mother's absence even more acute two years later, it doesn't change the fact that I volunteered to help Mariah out, and I have to finish what I started.

Inside the house, I meet Mariah's older brother Forrest who looks every bit like a mountain man with his full beard and red plaid shirt layered over a heather grey shirt. Mariah tells me he's only 32, but the beard makes him look much older.

He came in with a woman named Summer who is renting one of the cabins only to discover she had no idea how to work a wood stove. And with her friend a no-show, Forrest invited her to join the family for dinner instead of spending Christmas Eve alone. His dog Bodhi, a German Shepherd mix, sits on the floor next to the chair.

While we make our way to our seats at the table, I realize this is showtime. This is when Emily will probably interrogate Mariah and me. Suddenly I can barely keep myself calm, my mind going a mile a minute. What did we agree on during the drive here? Where was our first date? I'd been so casual then, whipping out the answers like candy, thinking this whole thing was nothing but fun and games.

Only it's not funny anymore. And it stopped being a game the moment we kissed.

Dinner begins fifteen minutes later, and Mariah and I sit next to each other. Across the table in front of us sit Emily and Brad while Jonathan is seated on a baby seat between them. With Mariah's parents seated at the head of the table, Forrest and Summer are seated next to me, while Harper sits next to Mariah. Just as she'd warned me earlier, her youngest sister is already filming everything with her phone on a self-stabilizing selfie stick. Her first order of business is the food as she orders us not to touch any of the dishes yet.

I turn to look at Mariah, who's stifling a giggle. "You weren't kidding. She's a pro."

Harper shushes everyone. "Chin out, stomach in, wet your lips. And no looking at the camera."

"You heard her," Mariah whispers as she fights hard not to laugh. "Now act normal."

Christmas Eve dinner for the Peters residence is a smorgasbord of dishes from roast turkey with cornbread and walnut stuffing, Christmas ham with pineapples, sweet potato casserole with marshmallows on one side and plain on the other (apparently to appease the siblings, the girls who like having the marshmallow on top and Forrest who prefers it without), cranberry sauce, and persimmon pudding. There are other dishes, too, like green bean casserole, pecan pie that's warming in the oven, and a gingerbread house Jonathan and Brad assembled earlier. It's enough food to feed over twenty people, but Mariah tells me it'll also serve as tomorrow's leftovers because no one will be slaving away in the kitchen then.

"Except to make fresh coffee," Forrest says. "You gotta have fresh coffee."

"You also don't want to have us do the cooking," Emily says. "That's why Mom and Dad kick us out of the kitchen ever Christmas."

"We're good at many things, just not cooking," Harper says, laughing.

"Forrest is actually the best cook out of all of them," Brad says as Emily glares at him. "Hey, it's the truth."

"How long have you known my daughter, Logan?" Mariah's mom asks after everyone loads their plates with food. "Oh, and call me Harmony."

"I've known Mariah three years, Mrs... er, Harmony," I reply, feeling everyone's eyes on me.

"Where'd you guys meet?" Emily asks.

"At a cocktail networking event sponsored by some local business," Mariah replies. "I was there to promote the shop."

"And my brother and I were representing our repair shop, Garrison Motors."

"Repair shop, eh?" Ewan' eyes narrow. "You, by any chance, know anything about classic cars? Trucks, maybe?"

"I may be handy around the lodge but I'm hopeless when it comes to engines," Forrest says before turning to Summer to see if she needs anything. Behind him, Bodhi lifts his head before setting it back down between his paws.

"Cars, trucks, motorcycles. They all need engines to run, sir," I say. "I'd love to check out your truck."

He smiles. "Hope you don't mind me picking your brain tomorrow then."

"Definitely not."

"Can't wait till you drive my baby around town," Ewan adds as he rubs his hands together.

"There goes Dad," Mariah says, laughing. "Prepare to get dirty then."

I grin. "No problem."

"Was it love at first sight?" Harper asks. "I love those kinds of stories. It just makes the romantic in me swoon. I can't wait to fall in love."

"You're too busy looking at your phone to fall in love, honey," Harmony says as Harper rolls her eyes. "Who knows? The man for you just might be standing in front of you, and you'd never know it because you're always on your phone."

"If it happens, it happens," Harper declares. "He's just not here yet. But when he does show up, I'll know because it'll be a knock-your-socks-off type of falling in love."

"Better get those socks ready then," Brad says.

Harper turns to face me. "Was it like that for you, Logan, when you saw my sister? Did Mariah knock your socks off?"

I can see Mariah's eyes widen as she stares at me, but I keep cool and nod. "Yes, she certainly did."

Harper giggles. "Ooh, tell us more."

"What made it love at first sight for you, Logan?" Emily asks as Mariah's face turns crimson. "It has always intrigued me over how men fall in love."

"Why don't you just ask me?" Brad asks, looking offended.

"Because you go all biology major on me, Professor Talbot," she replies. "I don't want to know about endorphins or serotonin levels. I want to know about the butterflies and the googly eyes."

"You could have just said so," Brad says, looking more offended than he did earlier, although, from the way he's grinning at his wife, he's really not. "I don't do the googly eyes, though. They're creepy." He crosses his eyes at her until she giggles.

"Guys, that's personal, isn't it?" Mariah says. "I'm sure Logan doesn't want to go into details about how he felt when we–"

"It was her smile," I begin as everyone at the table becomes silent, "and that dimple on her right cheek. And, of course, her eyes, especially when she's happy, whether she's arranging her flowers or when... she's with me. And then there's her laugh. She never fails to make my world brighter and lighter whenever she laughs."

Harper sighs heavily after a few moments. "That was... that was just beautiful."

"Three years is a long time to keep it all quiet, though," Emily says almost to herself before she looks at Mariah, her eyes narrowing. "How come you never mentioned him last year, Mariah? Or the year before? In fact, you never even told us you were seeing anyone."

"Because I didn't ask her out until six months ago. Until that moment, we were just friends. Business friends." My reply comes a little too fast, but I don't care. I can almost feel Mariah's panic flow right through me as she grasps my hand in a death grip under the table.

"And before I knew it, he asked me to marry him two weeks ago," Mariah says.

"And she said yes," I add as Mariah shows off a ring I unfortunately didn't pick out. But as the tiny diamond catches the light, I'm glad she's got great taste.

"That's pretty fast, isn't it?" Emily says. Mariah was

right to warn me about her. She sure plays the bad cop in the good cop/bad cop routine very well.

"Why not? I asked your mom to marry me after knowing her for two weeks," Ewan says, smiling as he gazes at his wife before looking at me from across the table. "But I totally get waiting for the right moment, Logan. All I want for my daughters is for them to find true love like I did with their mother. Two weeks, two months, two years. What matters is that you love my daughter, and she loves you right back."

Emily still doesn't look convinced. "I just can't understand why Mariah never said anything. Six months is also quite fast, don't you think?"

"Fast? We slept together two days after we met, and you said yes to me six months after that," Brad says, taking a sip from his beer and ignoring his wife's horrified gasp as she instinctively covers Jonathan's ears.

"Brad!"

Harper giggles, and I can feel a scuffle of feet under the table between her and Mariah.

Harmony kisses her husband on the lips while all her daughters cover their eyes in mock embarrassment. "Oh, honey bunny, if you hadn't asked me to marry you when you did, I would have done the asking. I wasn't about to let you go." They stop kissing to watch their daughters' expressions, laughing before kissing again as Brad and I laugh.

It's a dynamic I never saw with my parents, definitely not with Dad who slept around and even boasted about his conquests to his sons until the day we told him to get out of the house if he dared mention it again. It made Liam and me tight because we were all we had, along with Mom.

"Did I tell you they met at the first Burning Man event on Baker Beach in San Francisco?" Mariah asks me as I shake my head. "Mom was the total hippie while Dad was there with his buddies on break from the university. Total opposites."

"All you need is love," Ewan says. "And trust, and a little laughter along the way."

"I think the secret to marriage is to make life interesting for each other," Harmony says. "In today's world where there are no secrets, where everyone films everything..." She pauses to glare at Harper who lowers her selfie stick on the table. "You need to keep something just for the two of you. Something special. Something private."

Harper's face brightens. "You mean something kinky? BDSM, that kind of thing?"

Emily covers Jonathan's ears again. "Oh no, we are not letting this conversation go there. This is supposed to be a child-friendly Christmas, Harper, for crying out loud. Have some decorum!"

"I'm game if you are, love. You were always curious about it since that movie, Fifty Shades... something came out, and you thought the hero's butt looked hot," chimes Brad as Emily looks even more horrified.

Across the table, Forrest and Summer look on,

amused at the entire exchange, as Mrs. Peters clears her throat.

"How's Jonathan? Has he hit the terrible twos yet?"

As the conversation shifts to Jonathan's latest milestones, I focus on finishing the rest of my dinner. Awkward moments or not, Mariah's family seems fun and open with each other.

Her parents are a hoot, the serious-looking Ewan Peters with his thick glasses still evidently in love with his hippie wife with her bangles and love for anything patchouli. And her siblings, as different as they seem to be, with Emily being as uptight as Harper is easygoing, all get along. It's amazing to see just how much they all seem to love each other that they don't even have to say the words.

And maybe, when the company is just right, sometimes you don't have to.

After dinner, everyone helps with the cleanup. This is one area where Mr. and Mrs. Peters let their kids take over completely while they spend time with their grandson. I volunteer to help dry the dishes, but Mariah kicks me out of the kitchen.

"Girls only," she says as she playfully pushes me out of the kitchen and into the living room where Brad is sitting on the couch by himself. Forrest had left right after dinner, walking Summer back to her cabin and probably making sure she won't burn the house down trying to get the wood stove to work.

"That's the Peters sisters for you, man," Brad says as he hands me a beer. "They're tight even if they don't see each other all year. You never want to piss one off or you'll never hear the end of it from the others."

"That must have been an interesting reunion with…" I cock my head toward the direction of Elliot's house, "the guy next door."

Brad rolls his eyes. "Now that was a mess. I don't know what I'd have done if I discovered my fiancee cheating on me with my best friend, but Mariah handled it well. Gracefully, if I may say so. Hell, I know I wouldn't have." He glances at the door leading to the kitchen. "But the Peters sisters are one classy bunch."

"What happened?"

Brad studies my face, surprised. "You don't know? She didn't tell you?"

"Only that they broke up before the wedding."

"She walked in on them doing the nasty in their apartment," Brad whispers. "And to think that Minerva was her maid of honor and her best friend. Can you imagine recovering from that?"

"I'd have killed him."

Nodding, Brad takes a sip of his beer. "Em and I were already married then, and man, she was so mad for Mariah she could have gone over there and beat the crap out of Elliot herself. And poor Mariah was simply trying to keep calm because, hell, it was a huge wedding. Over three hundred guests, and pretty much, that's the town of Auburn Springs as it is." He takes a deep breath and sighs. "Where do you even start letting everyone know the wedding's off?"

"That's terrible."

"But Mariah's the epitome of class. While what's-his-face and Minerva hightailed it out of there, Mariah quietly informed everyone that the wedding was off and that was that. She didn't elaborate, just I'm-sorry-to-inform-you-that-the-wedding-has-been-canceled.   Oh, and return every single wedding gift that had already been delivered to the house."

"And now they're celebrating Christmas next door."

"I can't blame them for waiting to come back two years later," Brad says. "He and Mariah were childhood friends. His parents used to work at the lodge, but after what happened, they quietly resigned. They've resumed their friendship in the last year but it's different, you know? And it only makes things complicated."

"We ran into them earlier," I say, "while Mariah was giving me a tour of the place."

Brad laughs. "Did you punch him for me?" He pauses. "Just kidding, but you know what I mean, right? I'm glad Mariah's moved on, and this time, with someone who is actually cool."

I chuckle. "Why, thanks. I wouldn't want to know what would happen if I wasn't cool enough."

"You ride bikes. You repair them. You're a social media star," he says, patting my shoulder. "But the most important thing of all is that I've never seen Mariah happier than she looks now. She's practically glowing. And that makes you cool in my book. And in Em's book as well, even if she'll give you the third degree now and then. She's just being protective of her little sister."

"Nothing wrong with being protective." I take another swig of my beer.

"Have you decided on a date yet?"

Sputtering, I stare at him. "A date?"

Brad laughs. "A wedding date, man. What else?"

Crap. This conversation is definitely heading toward shaky ground. "We haven't gotten that far in planning a date yet. We're both busy... with our own businesses."

He peers at me. "You guys aren't planning on eloping, are you?"

"It hasn't crossed our minds, no."

"Because it's not going to look good for a florist to elope. Not good for business," he says. "Em and I did that, by the way. She initially wanted a grand wedding, but she was a grad student and I was a professor. The logistics just weren't there, especially since Mariah was scheduled to get married the same year, and someone told Em that it wasn't good to have sisters get married in the same year. Some superstition or something. So we ran off instead, even had an Elvis impersonator walk her down the aisle."

"And the family was okay with that?"

His voice lowers as he continues. "Are you kidding? Harmony was pissed. She had wanted her daughters to get married right here at the Soraya, garden wedding and all. Then Mariah's wedding was canceled, and Em and I eloped." He slaps my shoulder. "So it's safe to say the pressure's on, bud. All eyes are going to be on you two."

"Great." I chuckle dryly. For a serious-looking Biology professor, Brad's funny, but he could also be drunk. Still, he hasn't told any lies about anything, especially not the part where all eyes will be on Mariah and me from here on. It's enough to make me nervous.

"You'll do alright,"

When I say nothing, Brad holds up his hand to show off his wedding ring. "As for Em and me, the elopement went great. Going on three years and counting."

For a serious-looking Biology professor, Brad's funny, but he could also be drunk. But what he just said about all attention going to Mariah and me is enough to make me nervous. We're supposed to break up after this. That means another disappointment for Mr. and Mrs. Peters.

"Congratulations on three years," I say, clearing my throat.

"Thanks. So when do you think the wedding's going to be?" he asks as Jonathan appears, blond curls flying as he gleefully runs to his father with a wooden plane in his hand.

"Dada!"

As Brad sets down his beer to lift Jonathan in his arms, I realize I want this—all of this. I want a home and a family. And I want a woman like Mariah to share it with me.

But as Brad watches me, reality sets in, and I remember why I'm really here. I'm not here to want such things. I'm here only to fulfill a role, and so far, I'm floundering.

"We'll figure out a date soon and let you guys know," I say. "And I promise you, no eloping either."

Hell, there's not even going to be a wedding.

CHAPTER 7

Mariah

I'M GLAD MY SISTERS DON'T ASK ME ANY MORE questions about Logan. Instead, between glasses of wine while we rinse and put away the dishes, we talk about Emily's latest kitchen remodeling project to Harper's celebrity sightings.

It's a hodgepodge of topics that make me smile, bringing me back to the time when we were children, shifting from one topic to the next so fast it would make anyone's head spin. I'm glad not much has changed, even as we've all gone our separate ways and changed somewhat.

It also reminds me I need to hang out with them more often. But with Emily living in Colorado and Harper flitting from one party to the next—thanks to her job as a fashion and lifestyle vlogger—it's been tough. That's why we show up for Christmas.

When we emerge from the kitchen, my heart catches in

my throat when I see Logan sitting with my parents, Brad and Jonathan. He looks like he belongs, and I hate knowing that in a few days, I'm going to be telling them that Logan and I broke up. But I take a deep breath and force a smile as Logan sees me and gets up from the couch. This was my idea, and I have to go through with it until the end.

"How are you?" he asks when he reaches my side.

"It was wonderful catching up with everyone. What about you?" We're standing in the hallway leading to the guest room.

"Better now that you're here," he replies. "The questions were getting pretty intense."

I frown. "What type of questions?"

He shrugs. "Just the usual. How long we've been seeing each other. Have we set a date and all that."

I sigh. How come I'm not surprised? "I hope my family's not too crazy for you."

He laughs. "No, they're great, Mariah. They're actually fun to be around."

Suddenly Harper gasps as she turns to us. "Oh, look! You're both standing under the mistletoe."

"No, we're not," I blurt out before looking up and realizing how wrong I am when I see a mistletoe hanging above the hallway entrance. "Oh, crap."

How did I not catch that?

"It only means one thing," Brad says, grinning. "Time for a kiss."

As everyone hoots and hollers for a kiss, Logan turns

toward me, a faint smile on his lips. I can feel my cheeks burning, the realization that I'll be kissing Logan in front of my family for the first time making me want to blurt out the truth, that this is all a charade, and that there's nothing to see here.

But as Logan cups my face in his hands like he did when he kissed me on the bridge, I feel myself calm down. There's something about his touch that reminds me it's not all that bad, really. Okay, maybe pretending to be someone we're not is not exactly a good thing, but the kiss on the bridge certainly was. Just as the kiss that follows is as well. The touch of his warm lips on mine makes me forget everything else.

It makes me wish we really are a couple.

Then as quickly as the kiss comes, the moment is gone.

"There you go," Logan murmurs as he pulls away. "It's not so bad, is it?"

"No, it wasn't." I know I'm blushing, and my family's cheers are not helping at all. I've never been one to flaunt my relationships, and I'm definitely not flaunting one that's only going to last until the charade is over in two more days.

"We can always practice more later when there's no audience," Logan whispers.

My cheeks burn even more. "I'd like that."

"You guys are just the cutest," Harper says as she peers into her camera. "Can I post this online?"

I look at Logan. "We haven't told her we don't want our stuff online, have we?"

He shakes his head. "We better tell her now."

We make our way toward Harper who's standing by the Christmas tree. Just like the kiss on the bridge, the one under the mistletoe has left me feeling giddy and my stomach is still flipping nervous. Why do I feel like I'm back in high school and my crush just kissed me? It's bad enough that my crush never kissed me in high school because he never knew I was crazy for him to begin with.

But I'm no longer in high school. I'm home, and I'm staging a play in front of my family all because the man I once loved and my former best friend are spending Christmas next door, and I didn't want them to see I still had no one.

Harper thrusts the camera in front of us. "What do you guys think of this shot? I think it's perfect!"

I see Logan and me on her camera display, kissing under the mistletoe. It's such a perfectly timed shot that even I want to get my copy. I love the way she framed it, the way Logan cups my face, and how he made me feel safe with him.

"I think it's beautiful," I say as I squeeze Logan's hand.

"Is it okay if you don't post our photos online?" He asks as Harper looks up from her camera, surprised.

"Oh, okay."

"I'd love a copy, though," he adds. "Can you send one to Mariah, and she can send it to me?"

"Sure." Harper presses a few buttons. "Sent!"

I hear my phone beep, the photo appearing in my Messages. "Thanks, Harper."

"No problem," she says as she resumes taking pictures, this time of Jonathan sitting in a wooden rocking horse that Dad made back when Forrest was his age. We all rode on that thing at one time or another, and I have no doubt more of their grandkids will probably enjoy it just like Jonathan.

"Do you think she suspects?" I ask Logan a few minutes later.

He smiles as he tucks a lock of hair behind my ear. "What's there to suspect?"

The butterflies in my stomach flutter as I catch his gaze and I can't help but smile. "You're fantastic at this."

Logan's expression turns serious. "It's got nothing to do with that. I simply enjoy being around your family."

Half an hour later, Emily and Brad bid everyone goodnight as they make their way to the guest room, Jonathan asleep on Brad's shoulder. Harper puts on a pair of big white earphones, plops herself on the couch, and begins editing the pictures on her camera. My parents are busy rearranging the presents around the tree, placing Jonathan's present front and center so he can get to them first thing in the morning.

"Want to step outside for a few minutes?" I ask Logan.

"I'd love to."

Grabbing our coats, we step outside and stand by the

railing. Snow is still falling, and it makes for a perfect white Christmas.

Logan holds out his hand to catch a few snowflakes. "I can't believe how quiet it is out here."

"I love how quiet it becomes when it snows," I say.

"Why's that?"

"It's because snow is made of ice crystals which have space between them. The open spaces absorb sound waves, making everything seem quieter. The lighter and fluffier the snow, the better it is at absorbing those sound waves."

"Makes sense." Logan thinks for a few moments. "It's beautiful up here."

As I wrap my arms around myself, he pulls me next to him. He feels warm and secure, and I want nothing more than to rest my head on his shoulder.

"There's an apple tree over there," I say, pointing to the side of the house even though it's dark. "Some nights, you can hear deer come up and munch on the fallen apples. I used to lie in bed and listen until I'd fall asleep."

He chuckles. "A far cry from listening to the sounds of the city."

"It sure is."

"It's been so long since I've been back to Mount Baldy to remember how it feels like to live out in the boonies," he says. "Guess that makes me a city boy now."

I smile. "I guess it does."

When the cold finally makes its way through our

coats, we go back inside and welcome the warmth of the fire. But everyone seems to be heading to bed and as I make my way to the guest room, Mom calls my name.

"Where do you think you two are going?" She asks as we stop and face her.

"I'm taking Logan to the guest room."

"Not unless you want to inhale patchouli all night," Dad says. "Mom converted it into her blending room a year ago and there's no bed in there anymore. Just tables and shelves with her oils and stuff."

"You did put both your bags in your bedroom, right?" Mom asks and I nod.

"Aren't you worried about us staying in the same room?" I ask. "I remember when Em first brought Brad home, you didn't allow them to stay in the same room."

"That was then and this is now." Mom pauses, chuckling. "Besides, you two are engaged. I'm not about to pretend you've never done it before tonight."

"Mom!" I gasp in surprise as Dad chuckles.

"You two should be fine," he says,. "I added more pillows, just in case."

Mom yawns. "Good night, you two love birds." She gives me a hug, followed by Dad. "See both of you in the morning."

"Your mom and I have been up since five and now we're both pooped," he says, pausing. "Remember when we used to stay up late just so we could do the whole Santa delivering presents routine, Harmony?"

Mom laughs. "Remember when we used to make Santa's footprints coming from outside using flour?"

"Until I figured out it was flour by tasting it," Harper says as we laugh.

"With four kids and exchange students in the house, it was crazy keeping up the illusion."

Mom shoots him a glance. "It's not an illusion and you know it."

"Until they all hit their tweens and started questioning everything." Dad turns to face Logan and grips his hand. "I'm so happy you could join us for Christmas, Logan. There's nothing in the world that makes me happier than seeing my daughter in love. It's been a while since I've seen her smile."

"Dad, I'm right here. I can hear you," I say, sighing. I love them to bits, but sometimes, they drive me up the wall.

"Well, good night. Don't cause a racket," Dad says as Mom pulls him toward their bedroom playfully.

"Let them be, honey," she says, winking at us. "I'm sure Logan knows what to do."

"Mom!" But even as I protest, I know it's useless. If their goal was to embarrass prim and proper Mariah Peters, it worked. Even Logan is grinning from ear to ear as he watches me squirm.

"If you'd rather have me sleep somewhere else, I can take the couch downstairs. I know this wasn't part of the deal," he murmurs as the door at the far end of the hall opens, and Emily peers out.

Oh, crap! Did she hear him? Before Emily can say anything, I press against Logan and kiss him.

The kiss takes him by surprise, but only for a split second. He pulls me against his body and kisses me right back, his arms circling my waist. His lips are soft, his stubble scratching my skin. When he tugs on my lip with his teeth, it sends a wave of pleasure down my spine.

As I hear a door closing, I know I should pull away, but I don't. I don't care that the time for pretense is over. Instead, I give that kiss everything I have, and I'm glad I'm not alone. Logan pulls me closer, our tongues melding together as if he can't bear to stop now, either. When he releases my lips, I'm breathless, his mouth trailing down my jaw to my neck. Then he returns to my lips again, his tongue slipping between my teeth.

Logan reaches for the doorknob behind me and twists it open. As the door opens, we stumble inside my bedroom, our lips still locked together. It's as if we're starving, our kiss deepening as our hands move hungrily against skin, gliding over shoulders and backs, fingers catching in our hair.

I should stop this, but I don't want to. Logan makes the butterflies in my belly flutter like crazy. His kiss makes me go weak in the knees. His erection straining inside his jeans and pressing against my belly makes me feel giddy with excitement and desire. It's everything I've ever dreamed of—Logan wanting me right back—but it's the very thing I'm also afraid of. I don't want to feel this good only to watch things fall apart again as it did with Elliot.

Doesn't everything happen that way?

I pull away, out of breath, my cheeks burning. "I'm... I'm sorry, Logan. I shouldn't have kissed you like that."

As he pulls away, there's no mistaking the bulge in his jeans. "Don't be sorry."

"This... I just made everything complicated."

"Do you want us to stop?" he asks.

"No, but we have to."

Logan lifts my hand to his mouth. His lips feel soft and warm against my knuckles, and I want so much for him to kiss me on the lips instead and forget what I just said.

He clears his throat. "Why don't we figure out our sleeping arrangements?"

I force myself to look around my old bedroom, from the pink curtains covering the windows to the off-white color I'd painted the walls two years ago, right after I called off the wedding and came up here to be with family. White walls to signify starting over, even though I never really did. I simply tucked all my feelings inside and buried myself in painting everything white and making one floral arrangement after another, providing every couple with an experience I never got to see for myself.

As my gaze leaves the walls and moves toward the bed, I gasp.

"What's wrong?" Logan asks as I point to the bed.

CHAPTER 8

Logan

So what if it's a twin-size bed? Nothing to be alarmed about.

Yeah, right.

It's everything to be alarmed about, especially given that the mere closeness of Mariah is sending my senses into overdrive. My nerves are on fire just by being close to her, and when she's pressed against me, I can barely think straight.

When she kissed me again just outside the door, I did everything I could to throttle the dizzying current racing through me, but it was no use. It's as if Mariah's unlocked every emotion I've long kept under wraps because our friendship was more important.

"Do you think we'll be okay?" Mariah asks. "I have a sleeping bag in the closet. I could take that out."

I shrug. "If you prefer it that way, sure, but it's really

no problem, Mariah. Seriously. I just want you to be fine with it."

She bites her lip. "Of course, I'm fine with it. We're friends."

Tightness grips my chest at the last word but I force a smile. "I'll make sure not to hog the bed."

"I know you won't." Mariah becomes serious as she tucks a lock of her hair behind her ear. "I'm so sorry about this, Logan. I really thought my mother would put us in separate rooms like she did with Emily and Brad."

I chuckle. "Maybe she didn't want to jinx the engagement."

"Knowing her, you're probably right." Her brow furrows as a thought comes to her. "Come to think of it, I bet she put crystals under the bed, too. Maybe that's what they were doing my sisters and I were in the kitchen."

She could be right. They had been absent while I was talking to Brad, and I simply assumed they were playing with their grandson.

I exhale. "Only one way to find out."

We get down on our knees next to the bed and she lifts the bed skirt. Sure enough, there's a grouping of crystals of various sizes and colors on the floor underneath.

"I can't believe it," she murmurs, pointing to the crystal closest to her. "This is rose quartz, and over next to it are rhodochrosite, garnet, carnelian, Amazonite...

and I think that last one is malachite. Don't ask me what they do exactly, but I think they're known as relationship stones."

"What makes you say that?"

"She used to recommend them to couples."

I help her up from the floor. "Your mom's definitely not taking any chances, then. Do those things even work?"

I sure hope none of them are designed to increase one's sex drive because I can barely contain my reaction to being close to her. It's bad enough that my self-control to kiss her again may not hold up till the morning, not if we have to sleep on a twin-sized bed at that.

"I have no idea." Mariah frowns. "I only know what they are because I used to be in charge of the gift shop, and we sold tons of them. Necklaces, bracelets, and just the stones themselves, unpolished. They were also fun for wire-wrapping projects during nature camps."

"Seriously, Mariah, I can sleep somewhere else if that makes you feel–"

"No! Don't be ridiculous, Logan. We'll be fine," she says, chuckling. "At least you can't say my parents are predictable."

"No, they're definitely not." They're definitely modern if it doesn't bother them we'd sleep in the same bed. In fact, they're encouraging it.

"The last time Elliot spent the night here when their house was being renovated, she told him to sleep in the…" Her voice fades as if she just realized what she just said. "I'm sorry. I shouldn't bring him up all the time."

"Don't be." But even as I say it, I can't help but remember what Brad told me about how Mariah had kept it all together after discovering her fiancé and best friend's betrayal. It would have been around the time we met which made sense.

Looking back, Liam and I had already known her then. We even knew about the engagement because Mariah wore a ring—a huge rock, at that. And then, one day, the ring was gone, and there was no mention of a wedding. Liam and I were still reeling from our mother's loss to do or say anything. If Mariah had wanted us to know what had happened, she'd have told us, but she didn't. And I can't blame her. Some wounds are just too deep to share.

As we stand in front of each other, I want so badly to cup her face in my hands and kiss Elliot out of her system. I want to show her that not all men are like that asshole next door. But I can't do that. Mariah's vulnerable. And judging from the turmoil of emotions I'm going through, I just might be, too.

"Guess we better get to bed," she whispers.

"I'll use the bathroom in the hallway." I grab my backpack and step out of the room, my heart racing. Today has been a day filled with new experiences, from being around a family that unabashedly loves each other to the practice kiss on the bridge that takes the top spot. But I've never felt so conflicted. I want to give Mariah everything, yet I know I can't, not right now. I need to focus only on what she needs me for and wait until everything is over before we can take any of this further.

"Everything alright?"

I turn to see Harper coming up the stairs behind me.

"Of course. I would it be?"

She shrugs. "Honestly, you guys looked like you were scared to death at the prospect of sharing a bed."

I laugh, hoping not to betray my nervousness. "That's so not the case."

"But I could be wrong. I bet it must be nerve-racking meeting us for the first time. We can be over the top sometimes," she says.

"It was at first, but you guys made it fun."

"I'd be excited if Mom and Dad would let my boyfriend and I sleep in the same bed, much less the same room. But that would mean I'd need to get a boyfriend first." She sighs. "Difficult to do when you're traveling as much as I do."

"Is there anyone you particularly like among your friends?"

Harper thinks for a few moments and shakes her head. "No one."

"Then maybe you haven't met him yet," I say, grinning.

"You're right." Her expression turns serious as she continues, "I just hope you don't break her heart like Elliot did."

My throat tightens. That's exactly the plan even

though it's the last thing I want to do when this charade is all over. "I'd... never do that."

"Promise?"

The door opens and Mariah pokes her head out. "Oh, hi, Harper. I thought I heard you out here. What's up?"

"Just chatting with Logan here," she replies, grinning. "Making sure he doesn't break your heart."

Mariah's face pales but only for a moment. "There are no guarantees in this world, Harper."

Her sister rolls her eyes. "Oh, come on, Mariah. I'm just kidding."

"And I'm going to brush my teeth," I say before making my way to the end of the hall before any of them can reply.

❄

"I'm sorry if Harper harassed you out there," Mariah says when I return to the bedroom. "She can be pretty outspoken sometimes."

"I'm a big boy. I can take care of myself," I say as I close the door behind me. "It's okay, Mariah. Really."

As she pulls up the covers and slides underneath, she looks adorable in a pink pajama set with reindeer and snowmen all over. "Is she still out there?"

"She went back to the living room and is now working on her laptop."

"She'll probably be up a while then," Mariah says as I

set my backpack next to the dresser and walk to the bed. With her hair splayed on the pillows, she's breathtaking and it will take all my willpower to be good tonight.

Good as in keeping my hands to myself.

I'm just glad I remembered to pack a pair of flannel pants and a t-shirt this morning since I normally sleep with only boxers on. Hell, sometimes nothing at all.

As I slide under the covers, it's hysterical seeing the ocean of space between us as Mariah clings to the side of the bed for dear life.

"You comfortable over there?" I ask, grinning.

"Not really. I might fall over if I fall asleep."

"Then come here. I don't bite... well, unless you want me to."

She arches an eyebrow. "That's not helping, Logan."

"Come here," I murmur, serious this time as I shift away from the edge of the bed, and she does, too, sliding her head over my arm on the pillow. My pulse pounds the moment her body presses against mine but I force myself to relax.

"Just know I'm not going to touch you... not in any way you don't want me to," I murmur. "Just as we agreed."

She nods. "Just as we agreed."

We don't speak for the next few minutes even as the tension builds between us. Her breath feels warm against the hollow of my neck where she's nestled her head against my shoulder. Her hair smells of lavender and oranges.

"You feel good," she murmurs as she rests her hand against my chest. "Your pecs are so hard–"

I clear my throat. The way her voice lowered just now is sending signals down my body, right where I don't want them to. "That's not helping, Mariah."

"Sorry." She pulls her hand away but I grasp it and keep it there, warm and soft.

"Doesn't mean I don't like it."

"But your pecs are hard," she murmurs, smiling. "It's just an observation."

"Why, thanks," I say, grinning. "You feel really good, too. Soft and–"

"That's not going to help us either, Logan."

I chuckle. "It was just an observation."

As Mariah makes herself comfortable in my arms, I force myself to think of other things like truck engines and motorcycles. Anything to keep my mind off the fact that there's a gorgeous woman in my arms and all I want to do is kiss her and make love to her. The signals have all been there, the push and pull between us, the clenching of my belly and the rush of blood where it shouldn't be going if I'm to remain just her friend.

But that's the problem—I don't want to be just her friend anymore. I want to be so much more.

But what if I've been reading the signals all wrong? What if Mariah wants us to remain friends after this?

How'd I go from having full control at the beginning of the day to this? But I also don't want to trade this moment for the world even if it may end up being an uncomfortable night sleeping on a bed that's too narrow for two people who aren't exactly sleeping together.

I clear my throat and she looks up. "If, in the night, my hand ends up where it's not supposed to be... just a brush or something, just know that it's not intentional."

"No problem," she says as she shifts positions, doing her best to position her upper arm comfortably. When her hand brushes against my thigh, she freezes. "Sorry. Not intentional."

"That's okay."

"Maybe if I just turn the other way?"

As she rolls onto the other side, facing away from me, the scent of her hair and the feel of her body pressing against mine assails my senses.

"Is that okay?" she asks and I grunt yes. *Think of engine transmission systems, Logan.*

She doesn't speak for a few moments. Then she giggles. "Guess I'm your little spoon now."

I grin, taking in the scent of her hair as she settles into her pillow. I want her to be my little spoon every night. Hell, she can even be the big spoon if she wants to.

As Mariah turns her head to look at me, I do my best to focus on everything else but the feel of her body against mine. She's so soft and warm, the desire to tighten my hold of her body growing with every passing second.

"Thank you, Logan," she whispers. "Thank you for being here."

"I wouldn't want to be anywhere else," I murmur. "I love your family."

"I do, too." She smiles. "Merry Christmas."

I want to kiss the back of her neck, murmur in her ear, and assure her that no one will ever hurt her like Elliot did. I want to kiss her and make her forget the pain of his betrayal.

But I don't.

"Merry Christmas." I nuzzle my face in her hair instead. "We better get to sleep or we'll end up on Santa's naughty list."

She takes a breath as if about to say something but relaxes. "You're right. Good night, Logan."

I take one more whiff of her hair, at the same time pushing away thoughts that would definitely cross the friend zone line. "Good night, Mariah."

CHAPTER 9

Mariah

I'VE FORGOTTEN HOW IT FEELS TO WAKE UP IN someone's arms, but this morning, I'm reminded of how good it feels. Considering it's Logan, it's even better than I ever imagined. With his arms circled around my waist, his face nuzzled in my neck, his breath warming my skin, it feels... amazing.

I probably haven't moved an inch since I closed my eyes last night, afraid that if I did, he'd pull his arm away or worse, one of us would roll off the bed. But we're still here, nestled under the covers and, in my case, pretending to be asleep even as my body yearns for more of his touch. Maybe a kiss, just like the one yesterday.

Stop it, Mariah. Yesterday was a practice kiss, nothing more.

But as the sun's rays slip between the curtains, casting the bedroom in a soft ethereal glow, I also know that practice kiss or not, the sensations that came after had nothing to do with the charade we both find ourselves in.

Why do I keep denying that I've liked Logan for some time now? That I anticipate seeing him walk through the door of my shop every Friday morning to pick up the hand-tied floral arrangement I make for his mother, the one with her favorite flowers I know by heart. Pink Asiatic lilies, purple daisy poms, and alstroemeria with white waxflowers and purple statice.

Logan stirs behind me, his arms tightening as I press myself against him. I feel his body respond, the warmth of his lips brushing against the back of my neck, his stubble tickling my skin. There's another reaction, too, pressing against the back of my thigh.

Suddenly Logan stiffens, and he shifts his body away. "Sorry."

I grab his arm, keeping it where it wrapped around my waist. "It's okay, really. You feel good." *It's also been over two years since I've been really held by someone like this*, I almost add.

"You sure?"

"Yes, I am."

"Hang on," he murmurs, shifting his shoulder underneath my head. "I'm afraid my other arm's asleep."

I lift my head up as Logan slides his arm from under my head and straightens and bends it, bringing back the circulation. "You could have just removed your arm last night, Logan. No sense in giving up an arm for me."

He chuckles as he opens and closes his fist. "Nah, you're worth it."

His phone buzzes on the bedside table, and I hand it to him. He slides his arm under my head again while his other hand holds the phone. "It's Liam wishing us a Merry Christmas. I'll text him back later."

"You can text him right now if you want."

Logan stares at me for a few moments, then he shakes his head. "I see the guy every day."

He hands me his phone, and I set it back on the bedside table. "What are you looking at?" I ask when I turn to face him again and he's still gazing at me.

"Has anyone ever told you how beautiful you are?"

"Not recently."

"Then I'm telling you right now. You're beautiful, Mariah Peters."

"Thanks." I lower my gaze, my cheeks burning. "Be careful though."

"Why?"

"I just might believe you're serious."

My heart drums in my chest as Logan strokes my cheek. There's almost a sad look in his eyes and I wish I hadn't said what I'd just said. "Don't let one man's betrayal ruin the power of an honest compliment, Mariah."

His words hit me hard, like a freight train barreling

through my chest and then my heart. He's right, though. I've used Elliot's betrayal like a shield for so long that I've forgotten what it feels like to be vulnerable. To accept something as simple as a compliment spoken in earnest.

"Thank you," I murmur as I allow myself to enjoy the roughness of his fingers against my cheek and the softness of his gaze on my face.

"You're welcome." His voice reverberates in the space between us. It's lower, more controlled, and I see his Adam's apple bob as he swallows. "I loved sharing the bed with you."

I smile. "I did, too. I love that you made sure I wouldn't fall off the bed."

He thinks for a few moments. "That I made sure of although there are other ways of falling."

My chest tightens again. "You mean like falling in love?"

Logan clears his throat. "Something like that."

"Anyone you fall in love with is going to be one lucky woman."

He doesn't say anything for a few moments, his gaze intent as he strokes my cheek with his finger. "What if I already have?"

My throat tightens as the feel of his fingers on my skin sends my heart hammering against my chest. "Then I'm jealous of her."

"You don't have to be."

He gazes at me for what seems like forever before he leans in and captures my lips in a gentle kiss. It starts slow, his lips moving softly against mine, exploring, learning. But soon the kiss deepens, becoming more intense as his hand slides around my waist, pulling me closer to him. I moan softly into the kiss, my hands finding their way into his hair as I respond in kind.

The world fades away as we become lost in the moment, lost in the feel of each other. His lips move down my neck, nipping and kissing along the sensitive skin, sending shivers down my spine. My fingers grip his hair tighter as I arch into his touch.

We finally pull away, both of us breathing heavily. Logan rests his forehead against mine, his eyes closed as he tries to regain his breath. "God, Mariah," he whispers. "I've wanted to do that for so long."

I smile, my heart pounding in my chest. "Me too."

Logan pulls back and looks at me, his eyes searching mine. "I don't want to rush anything. I don't want to ruin our friendship."

I nod, feeling the same way. "Me, too."

"Maybe we should take our time?" he murmurs. "Go slow?"

I giggle. "Considering where we are right now, in a house full of people, that's a good idea."

He grins, leaning in to kiss me again just as someone knocks on the door.

"Everyone downstairs in five minutes," Mom says from outside the door. "It's Christmas morning and Dad made biscuits and gravy."

Like a spell broken, Logan leans back against the

pillows as we hear my parents saying good morning to someone outside the door while Jonathan happily shrieks downstairs.

"I do have to admit biscuits and gravy sure sounds good right about now," he murmurs as I slide off the bed.

"Guess it's time to go downstairs." I hurry into the bathroom, hoping he doesn't notice the blush that's crept all the way down my chest. Inside the bathroom, my heart races as I stare at my face in the mirror. I've always been called pretty... beautiful even. It was part of the package that was the Peters sisters.

But it wasn't all positive. With my blonde hair and blue eyes, Minerva once said it was like owning a permanent Fast Pass through life. But if that was the case, why did Elliot cheat on me with my best friend?

I close my eyes, remembering how Logan's arms felt as he held me, how his words felt so sincere.

Because they were, Mariah. You just refuse to believe it just like you've refused to believe every man who came along after Elliot.

I open my eyes, the truth right in front of me. Have I really been holding on to Elliot and Minerva's humiliation for the last two years? Have I been carrying it like a badge of honor all this time, a convenient piece of armor to protect me from falling in love?

I don't even have to answer that question. Of course, he's right. It's why I can't even accept a simple compliment, too worried that people only see the jilted bride from two years ago even though they probably don't even remember... or care. They probably just want me to move on and be happy. Isn't that why they're truly happy that I'm engaged again?

When I emerge from the bathroom, Logan is no longer in the bedroom. I hear him outside the hallway talking to Harper downstairs about joining everyone as soon as I'm ready. When he returns to the bedroom, I see that he's wearing a t-shirt under a red plaid shirt and blue jeans. A light beard darkens his jaw.

"You ready?" he asks, holding out his hand toward me. I'm ready as I'll ever be in a pink knit top with jeans even when there's really no need to get dressed up on Christmas morning, not at our house. Everyone will be wearing their PJ's to open their presents anyway, but with Logan being my fiancé, I also need to appear presentable, especially if Harper is filming.

We make our way down the stairs, my two sisters sitting on the floor in front of the tree. Little Jonathan is surrounded by presents of different sizes, and judging by the toys scattered around him, he's gotten a head start opening a few presents already. There's a red ribbon stuck to the top of his head.

"Who's Cooper?" Emily asks as my heart skips a beat.

"What?"

"Your presents all say, *From Mariah and Cooper.*

Who is he?" She holds up one of my presents and as I stare at Logan, I realize I'd forgotten to change the labels.

"It's my middle name," Logan replies. "Logan Cooper Garrison. That's my full name."

"So what do we call you?" Harper asks. "Logan or Cooper?"

"Logan," he replies. "Cooper was a... a phase for Mariah. But that's over now."

"Logan Cooper Garrison. It's such a biker name," Harper says out loud. "I found you and your brother online. I can't believe you never said anything, Logan. You guys have, like, tens of thousands of followers!"

Logan shrugs. "That's my brother's doing. He's the one in charge of social media."

"I did see his girlfriend and you're right, Mariah," Harper tells me. "I'd be dead from her dagger eyes if I just looked at her man sideways."

Logan laughs. "She doesn't share."

"You're not supposed to be looking at someone else's man, Harper," Emily says warily. "You know the drill. We've been there, done that, remember? I mean, not you, but you know what I mean."

"I know, I know," Harper mutters as Emily shoots a glance at my direction. For the first time, I don't even care that they're referring to what happened to me and Elliot. I haven't thought about that since Logan's kiss yesterday.

And then that kiss this morning...

"Where's Forrest?" I ask, wondering where my older brother is off to again. He's always been the serious one of all of us, enjoying his time alone in the woods whenever he can together with Bodhi. Forrest is also the most adventurous of the Peters siblings, having joined the Marines right out of high school and after he got out, backpacked through Europe and Asia on his own for two years before returning home a few years ago. Since then, he and Dad have made so many improvements to the Soraya that he's the only one my sisters and I can think of who can run the place when Mom and Dad retire.

"Summer needed help with the darn wood stove again," Harper says. "The fire went out during the night and the poor girl was freezing when he checked on her this morning."

"Wanna bet she's from the city," Emily says. "She should have gotten one of the rooms in the main lodge."

"Fully booked," Brad says.

"I hope she's okay," I say.

"She'll be fine." Harper winks. "My spider senses have been tingling ever since she joined us for dinner last night. Forrest never invites anyone to dinner. I think he likes her."

"It's just dinner. After all, who wants to spend Christmas Eve alone, anyway?" Brad says, shaking his head as he gets up to head toward the kitchen.

"Did you see him this morning?" Harper asks, laughing. When I shake my head, she continues, "Well, best to keep it a surprise." She turns to everyone. "Don't say anything, okay?"

"What happened?" I ask as everyone around us exchange glances.

"Don't say anything," Harper says just as Mom enters the dining room carrying a plate stacked with pancakes.

"We've got all the leftovers from last night, although Dad made pancakes, just in case," Mom announces, waving her hand toward the table already laden with dishes from last night all warmed up. "It'll be buffet style like always. You guys know where the plates and silverware are."

"Coffee is coming up," Dad announces as he emerges behind her carrying a large percolator, Brad right behind him carrying the mugs and saucers. Logan leaves my side to help them set everything on the table.

"At least the storm has passed. Has Mariah shown you around the property yet?" Mom asks as Logan shakes his head.

"A quick one," he replies. "She took me to the gift shop."

"You should show Logan around, Mariah. Maybe pop into one of the cabins," Mom says. "They should be open."

"The A-frames?"

"Of course, she means the A-frames. It's wonderful for a little bit of privacy," Harper adds as I glare at her, but it's no use. She just makes a face at me before holding up her phone and snapping a picture of Logan and me.

"Presents or breakfast first?" Dad asks, and the verdict is a mixed bag, although it doesn't matter. Little Jonathan voices his answer with a shriek of happiness as he tears through every present he can find.

CHAPTER 10

Logan

FIVE MINUTES AFTER BREAKFAST, WE ALL gather in the living room for present opening. Mariah settles in front of me, her back against my chest, and I can't help but feel a mix of comfort and nervousness at our closeness. It's all part of the act, I remind myself, even as I enjoy the warmth of her presence.

"Hey, gorgeous," I murmur, planting a kiss on her cheek as I notice Emily watching us. I wonder if she suspects anything, but I push the thought aside, focusing on playing my part convincingly.

Mariah giggles in response, "Hey, handsome."

Harper raises her camera and starts snapping pictures. "You guys look too cute," she says, taking a few more shots. "Picture perfect."

I feel Mariah tense slightly at Harper's words, and I give her shoulders a gentle squeeze, hoping to reassure her. This charade is harder than I anticipated, and I find myself wishing, not for the first time, that it wasn't just pretend.

Ewan clears his throat, drawing our attention. "Time to distribute the presents. At least the ones that Jonathan hasn't opened yet."

He begins reading out the name on each present, handing them out as he goes. I watch as Mariah opens her first gift from Harper, a card containing two tickets to a Broadway play about the Founding Fathers.

"Those tickets are in demand, by the way," Harper says as Mariah hands the tickets to me. "You can even sell them for a few thousand dollars each. But I hope both of you can see the play instead."

"I will," Mariah says before catching herself. "I mean, we will."

I notice her slip and give her hand a subtle squeeze. We're in this together, after all.

Emily and Brad's gift is next, a coffee-table book featuring Georgia O'Keefe's paintings of flowers. Harmony has made Mariah a new batch of body oils with her favorite scents, while Ewan got us a local calendar.

"That way, you won't forget where you came from," he says. "The lodge is in there, too, by the way."

"Thanks, Dad," Mariah replies. "I should get a few more to hand out to clients down in LA."

As everyone shows off the presents they received,

Mariah hands me a small gift bag. "This one's for you," she says.

I look at her, pretending to look genuinely surprised. The bracelet from the gift shop. "Thank you, love."

As I unwrap it, I find a braided leather bracelet with a platinum washer stamped with the word 'Strength' along the middle. Just like I told her yesterday, it's perfect and exactly my style.

"I grew up with the local woman who makes it and Mom carries her stuff in the shop," she explains.

"I love it," I say as I slip the leather bracelet around my wrist. The weight of it feels right, and I'm struck by how well Mariah knows me, even as friends.

Feeling a surge of affection–and guilt for the deception we're maintaining–I reach for the gift I'd bought for her. "I got you something for Christmas, too," I say, pulling out a velvet pouch from my back pocket.

Her surprise is evident. "You didn't have to," she says.

"I wanted to," I reply, and it's the truth. Charade or not, Mariah is my friend, and I wanted to get her something special. After she left the repair shop yesterday, I'd rushed to the store to find her something. If I was going to pretend to be her fiance, I was determined to act like one.

I watch as she loosens the tie and retrieves a delicate gold necklace, her face lighting up.

"Logan, it's beautiful. Thank you," she says, her voice soft with emotion.

"Do you like it?" I ask, suddenly nervous about my choice.

She turns to look at me again, leaning closer. "Like it? I love it. Can you put it on for me?"

"Of course." As I take the necklace from her hand, she gathers her hair and lifts it up. My hands brush the back of her neck as I fasten the clasp, and I feel a jolt of electricity at the contact. This is dangerous territory, I think to myself, even as I lean forward to look at how the necklace sits. "Perfect," I say, and I'm not just talking about the necklace.

After opening all the gifts, we all sit at the table for breakfast, leaving the living room a mess of wrapping paper and ribbons while we eat. Forrest finally joins us, with his dog Bodhi sitting on the floor behind his chair. I notice everyone staring at him, except for Harper who's still smiling her Cheshire Cat smile.

"What?" Forrest asks, frowning.

"All right, I'm finally saying it," Ewan declares. "What happened to your beard?"

"I shaved it off."

"What happened to your hair?" Harmony asks. "It's neat all of a sudden."

"Harper gave me a haircut," he replies before looking at all of us. "Why are you all staring at me like that? Don't you guys like it?"

"Of course we do, son," Ewan says. "It's just... just a surprise, that's all."

"You look ten years younger," Emily says.

"What she really means is that she now looks older than you," Brad says before Emily whacks her husband on the arm playfully.

I chuckle at the family's banter, feeling both amused and a little out of place. It's moments like these that make me acutely aware of my role as an outsider, despite the warm welcome I've received.

After breakfast, Mariah and her sisters tackle the dishes while Brad tidies up the living room. Harmony disappears into her office to work on new blends for the coming year, and Ewan invites Forrest and me out to the garage to work on his truck.

I'm grateful for the distraction and the chance to bond with Mariah's father and brother. As we tinker with the engine, I find myself genuinely enjoying their company. Ewan's pride in his classic red truck is infectious, and I'm honored that he's sharing this with me.

Two hours later, we finally get the engine running. The excitement is palpable as Ewan sits behind the wheel, revving up the engine. I stand by the hood, double-checking everything, feeling a sense of accomplishment. It's a good feeling, being able to contribute something real amidst all the pretending.

When I head back into the house, I'm greeted by Mariah's bright smile. "Sorry it took a while," I say, aware that I must look a mess.

"You've made Dad so happy," she replies, and I feel a warmth spread through me at her words.

"I'm going to take a quick shower upstairs and we

can hang out and do whatever you want," I tell her. She gives me a quick kiss on the cheek before I make it up the stairs, and I hear Emily and Harper's playful hoots of approval. It's a stark reminder of the performance we're putting on, and I feel a twinge of guilt.

Clean and changed, I rejoin the family downstairs just in time to hear Ewan declare, "He fixed the truck, honey. What a Christmas present, eh?"

"Does that mean you approve of your soon-to-be son-in-law?" Harmony asks, and he nods.

"Approve? Of course I approve," he replies, laughing before turning to look at Mariah. "Now when's the wedding?"

I watch as panic flashes across Mariah's face. "You didn't spring twenty questions on him, did you, Dad?" she asks.

"Of course, I did, honey. It's what I do," he replies, grinning as Mariah stares at him in horror. "Ah, just kidding, Mariah. You're both adults, and you're both old enough to make a huge decision on your own. He asked you to marry him, you said yes, and that's good enough for me."

I feel a mixture of relief and guilt at Ewan's words. His approval means more to me than I expected, which only makes our deception feel worse.

"So when's the wedding?" Harmony asks, and I tense, wondering how Mariah will handle this.

"I... I honestly have no idea," Mariah replies. "He's got a shop and I've got a shop and we're both busy–"

"You better not elope," Harper interrupts. "Because I need to be your bridesmaid. Or your maid of horror. And I can help get you the best deals on everything."

Emily laughs. "Be careful, Mariah. That probably means she gets the rights to all the pictures and videos so she can post it on her social media."

"Just one. Or maybe two," Harper says. "Better yet, make it a destination wedding. That way, I can write the whole thing off."

"Why does it have to be a destination wedding?" Harmony suddenly asks. "Why not do it right here? I've always dreamed my daughters would get married right here at the Soraya. It's perfect for such an event, don't you think?"

I watch as Harmony wraps her arms around Mariah's waist, and I can see Mariah's throat tighten. "I know it's too rustic for your taste, Mariah, but why don't you and Logan think about it? No pressure at all."

No pressure at all, I think wryly. If only they knew. As I watch Mariah navigate this conversation, I'm struck by a realization: part of me wishes this wasn't just pretend. The thought catches me off guard, and I push it aside. We're here to help Mariah save face, nothing more.

But as I look at her, surrounded by her loving family, I can't help but wonder: what if? What if this wasn't just an act? What if I really was going to be a part of this warm, loving family? The idea is both thrilling and terrifying.

I shake my head slightly, trying to clear these

dangerous thoughts. We have a role to play, and I can't let my growing feelings complicate things. But as Mariah catches my eye across the room, giving me a small, grateful smile, I know it's already too late. This charade has become far more real than I ever anticipated, and I'm not sure how to handle it.

For now, though, I return Mariah's smile and nod slightly, silently reassuring her that I've got her back. Whatever happens, we're in this together. And as I rejoin the family's lively conversation, I try to push aside my conflicting emotions and simply enjoy this moment of belonging, however fleeting it might be.

When I make my way downstairs after taking a quick shower and changing to clean clothes, the living room is empty except for Harper who appears to be in the middle of a live stream. I bring my finger to my lips and point to the front door, not wanting to disturb her but she waves me to come closer.

"Hang on, guys," she says to the camera before turning to me. "I want you to meet my future brother-in-law. And guess who it is!"

I shake my head, wishing I'd told her to keep the engagement on the down low but it's too late for that.

She peers into her phone, reading what someone had written. "Yes, you're right. Logan Cooper Garrison of the Garrison Bros! He's engaged to my sister. Small world!"

"Where's everyone?" I ask.

Harper cocks her head to the front door. "Em and Brad and taking a nap with Jeremy and Mom and Dad are out driving around in the truck. Pretty much, everyone cleared out the moment Mom said something about you guys getting married here."

"She said what?"

"Right here at the Soraya," Harper says. "It'd be perfect, don't you think?"

Before I can say something, she turns her attention back to her phone, at the comments scrolling so fast on her display. "It would be awesome, yes! Our lodge is really beautiful. It's got this rustic charm to it, in a good way. Not in a selling something on Craigslist way." She laughs at her own joke before reading another comment. "Hell, yeah, I'd get married here myself if I could. I just have to find someone first, though."

I clear my throat. "Where's Mariah?"

"Outside," Harper replies, her attention still on her live stream. "Probably hyperventilating over what Mom said, which reminds me. You guys need to set a date already."

"Thanks," I mutter as she says my name again in response to a comment.

"Yup. That Garrison bro, the gorgeous one."

I make my way to the front door, wishing I could

stick my fingers in my ears and sing la-la-la so I don't hear what else she's saying. I should have told her not to broadcast the engagement last night.

Hell, if Mariah and I weren't in trouble before, we sure are now.

CHAPTER 11
Mariah

I'M SITTING ON THE PATIO, MY COAT WRAPPED tightly around me as I gaze out at the expanse of white that is the Soraya Lodge. The freshly plowed road and the cabins in the distance are a familiar sight, but today they feel alien, tainted by the weight of my deception.

As Logan shuts the door behind him, I don't turn to look at him. "We've got a problem," I say, my voice barely above a whisper.

"I heard," he replies, and I can hear the concern in his voice.

"Mom wants the wedding to be held here," I explain, the words tasting bitter in my mouth. "I had to get away from everyone because I was about to have a full-on anxiety attack if I stayed inside any longer. In case she'd start going into the specifics. Luckily, she and Dad went out for a drive." I pause, taking a deep breath before voicing the question that's been gnawing at me. "What am I supposed to tell her now?"

I half expect Logan to say 'the truth,' but he doesn't. Instead, he suggests we take a walk to calm down. As he takes my hand and leads me away from the house, I feel a mix of gratitude and guilt. He's been so patient, so supportive throughout this whole charade, and here I am, dragging him deeper into my mess.

As we walk, Logan tells me that Harper has announced our engagement to her followers in her live stream. My heart drops. "No, she did not!" I exclaim, horrified. "I'm so sorry, Logan. I can't believe this is happening. This was supposed to be simple. Just a quick in and out, and no one would be none the wiser."

"You clearly underestimated your family, Mariah," Logan says gently. "They are clearly very excited for you. And thrilled."

His words, meant to be comforting, only make me feel worse. "But they're taking it too far," I protest weakly.

We continue walking, and I try to push down the rising panic. In the distance, I see families enjoying the snow, their laughter a stark contrast to the turmoil in my heart. Logan squeezes my hand, assuring me that things will be okay, but I'm not so sure.

As we walk, I start pointing out places where my siblings and I used to play. Talking about the lodge, about my family's accomplishments, helps lift my mood a little. For a moment, it almost feels like Logan and I are just friends again, exploring the property together. But there's an undercurrent of tension, a new layer to our dynamic that I'm not sure how to navigate.

We stop at the A-frame cabins, and I lead Logan to the one named Cercis. As I unlock the door and step inside, memories flood back. I tell Logan about the cabin's history, about the drawings I made that still hang on the walls. His compliment on my art brings a small smile to my face, but it's quickly replaced by a nervous energy as I realize how alone we are.

The air between us feels charged, filled with unspoken words and suppressed feelings. When Logan says I'm perfect just the way I am, I feel a blush creep up my cheeks, and I look away, suddenly overwhelmed.

"Want to head back to the house?" Logan asks, but I shake my head. Despite the cold, I'm not ready to face my family again. "Would you mind if we stayed here awhile?"

Logan takes a step towards me, concern in his eyes. "You're cold."

"We can start a fire," I suggest, my voice barely above a whisper.

"I'm afraid we started one before now," Logan replies, his voice low and intense. "But you're right. We should."

"A real fire," I clarify, my heart racing.

"Yes. A real one," he agrees, and suddenly the air between us feels electric.

I start rambling about the cabin's history, desperate

to fill the silence, to distract myself from the way Logan is looking at me. But when he tucks a lock of my hair behind my ear, I can't help but lean into his touch.

"I don't want to pretend anymore," I whisper, biting my lower lip as I rest my hand on his chest. "Definitely not right now."

"I don't want to either," Logan replies, his voice husky.

"I want everything on the table for us right now, Logan," I say, my voice trembling. "But only if it's real."

"It's always been real, Mariah," he murmurs, and then we're kissing.

The kiss is everything I've been yearning for - passionate, desperate, real. Logan's arms around me feel like home, and for a moment, I let myself believe that this could be our reality.

But then Logan pulls away, and reality comes crashing back.

"Mariah, we need to talk," he says, his voice serious.

My heart sinks. "What about?"

Logan takes a deep breath. "When we get back to the house, we need to tell them the truth. I mean it. If this is how we feel for each other, I want no more pretense between us, no more games."

I feel my body go cold, and it has nothing to do with the winter air. "I can't do that," I say, my voice barely above a whisper.

"Why not?" Logan asks, his brow furrowing. "Then we don't have to hide anything from them. I like you. In fact, I more than like you, and what's happening between us shouldn't be done under a charade."

I shake my head, panic rising in my throat. "You mean, tell them I lied about you being my fiancé? I can't do that."

"Why not?" Logan presses. "You can tell them I'm your friend and it's true. It's certainly a better story than telling them I'm some escort you hired off the Internet. Or worse, I'm filling in for the escort you hired off the internet."

I don't answer right away. The shame and fear I've been trying to ignore are threatening to overwhelm me. "Haven't you seen how happy we've made them?" I finally manage. "My parents love you... us. I can't ruin that now."

Logan's eyes soften, but his voice remains firm. "They love a version of us that's not real, at least not yet. Worse, they love a version of me that's not real. It's me, yes, because I sure haven't lied about the way I feel for you, but it doesn't change the fact that the fiancé you brought home with you is a fabrication, a made-up story so you could prove to your ex-boyfriend—not your family, but your ex-boyfriend and your former friend who have only seen us once—that you've moved on... that you're not alone anymore."

He pauses, and I can see the hurt in his eyes. It makes my chest ache.

"But the problem is," he continues, "Elliot and Minerva aren't the ones enduring the lie. It's your family. Can't you see, Mariah? The longer we keep this up, the more you're proving them right, that you haven't moved on at all."

His words hit me like a punch to the gut. I feel my defenses rising, my hands balling into fists at my sides. "You're wrong," I say, my voice tight with emotion. "I have moved on."

Logan shakes his head, frustration evident in his voice. "How can you say that when you can't even admit to yourself that this charade is wrong? Even you know it or you wouldn't have panicked after your mother suggested we get married right here."

He pauses, rubbing the back of his neck. When he speaks again, his voice is softer, almost pleading. "But that's what I'm telling you right now, Mariah, and I'm telling you this as your friend, as someone who's known you for the last three years and have always admired you... as someone who's always liked you more than you know. Let's come clean to them. They're your family."

"But I can't, not on Christmas Day," I say, clinging to any excuse I can find. "Not when we're leaving tomorrow and then all this will be over."

Logan's next words cut deep. "It's never going to be the same between us from this moment on, Mariah. You do know that, right?"

I don't answer. I can't. Instead, I draw the curtains close and head outside, waiting for Logan to follow. As soon as he steps out, I lock the door behind him, as if I could lock away the truth of what just happened.

"You don't think they'll be disappointed when you tell them we broke up?" Logan asks. "Will you tell them I cheated on you just like Elliot did?"

His words sting, and I lash out. "Is that all you're worried about? Your reputation?"

But Logan's response leaves me speechless. "You can ruin my reputation all you want, Mariah, I don't care. But it'll never change the fact that you refuse to move on after what Elliot and Minerva did two years ago. And I'm sorry that they did what they did, but there are better things to do than wallow in the past."

I clench my jaw, fighting back tears. I want to scream at him, to deny everything he's saying. But I can't, because deep down, I know he's right.

"I'm heading back to the main house," I announce coldly, unable to bear his presence any longer. "If you want to come along, fine. If you don't, fine."

As I walk away, I hear Logan's phone ring. He answers it, and I feel a surge of irrational anger. How dare he act so normal when my world is falling apart?

With each step back towards the house, I feel the weight of my lies pressing down on me.

How did the fairy tale end so quickly? One minute, everything was perfect and the next, we're no longer on the same page. Yet even though Logan is right – this charade is all wrong – why quit now when there are less than 24 hours left before we leave? This time tomorrow, we'll be on our way to LA, and a week from now – orat the rate things are going, even sooner – I'll let everyone know that Logan and I broke up.

He doesn't even have to do a thing. This is all on me.

"I'm going to spend a few hours with Chad," he says when he catches up with me. "I think it will do us both some good to be away from each other for a while. I'll be back tonight."

"Fine," I snap, still walking. I shouldn't be upset that he's leaving, but I am. What will my family say when they see he went out on his own without me?

"Mariah, stop," Logan says. "Let's talk."

I stop and turn to face him, forcing myself to focus on what I need to get off my chest. Logan's barely broken a sweat, still as handsome in his jacket and jeans, his hair hidden underneath a hand-knit wool cap.

"What's there to say? You've made up your mind to hang out with your friend, so do it. I'll manage on my own," I say. "Besides, what exactly is there to talk about, Logan? You said everything you wanted to say back at the cabin."

"Which part? The one where I told you it's time for us to come clean to your family or the part where I want us to start from the beginning because I meant both of them," he says. "I want to see you again, Mariah, but not with a lie hanging over our heads."

I shake my head. "The things you said back there about Elliot and Minerva and that I'm stuck in the past... they weren't exactly nice."

"But it was the truth." He looks around us before

taking a deep breath. "We need to be honest with each other."

"By telling me I'm stuck in the past?" I scoff. "That's not being honest, Logan. That's being cruel."

"That's because the truth can be cruel. It's not all fun and games, and right now, that's what this is for you. Fun and games. And for what? So that guy and his wife over there can see that you're not alone two years after he did what he did to you?" He shakes his head. "What do you want me to do, Mariah? Would you rather I lie to you just to make you feel better?"

I cross my arms in front of my chest. "You were fine lying to my family the entire weekend."

He laughs dryly. "We were both lying to your family, Mariah, about us. But you know what? I never lied about the way I felt about you."

I hear his words, but my anger refuses to let me take it in. "Yeah, right. Anyway, I'm going inside."

I head toward the direction of the house, not waiting for Logan to catch up. Let him hang out with his friend, Chad or whatever his name is. Let him do whatever it is he wants to do, I don't care. I just want to get this visit over with before Mom and Dad start making arrangements for a wedding that will never happen.

CHAPTER 12

Logan

As Mariah walks away, her cold dismissal stings more than I care to admit. I want to call her back. Maybe we can still salvage whatever's left of our friendship and this charade, but just then, my phone beeps again. I glance down to see my brother's text message pop on the screen.

> LIAM:
>
> You're engaged??? To Mariah???
> Since when???

I exhale. So he really did hear about it. And I haven't even texted or called him back to wish him a Merry Christmas since his message this morning. I'd been too distracted.

And now I'm in trouble.

LOGAN:

It's complicated.

After sending my response, I set my phone on Silent and slip it back into my pocket just as it rings this time. I heave a sigh of relief to see that it's not Liam.

It's my buddy Chad, and in a few words, I arrange for him to pick me up. I need some space, some time to clear my head after everything that's happened.

Twenty minutes later, I'm stomping my boots on the doormat outside the house. "Chad should be here in a few minutes," I call out as I step inside. But the words die in my throat as I see a stranger standing by the Christmas tree.

Blond hair, blue eyes.

My throat tightens. This must be Cooper, the real fake fiancé.

"Hey, man, I thought your flight was grounded," I say slowly, my mind racing to salvage the situation.

"It was, but I'm here now," Cooper replies, frowning. "Who are you?"

"I'm Logan. Mariah's... friend."

Cooper's eyes narrow. "That's not what I've been hearing."

The tension in the room is palpable. I can see the confusion and disappointment on everyone's faces, especially Mariah's parents. Emily is glaring at Mariah, while Harper seems caught between shock and amusement.

Mariah steps in between us, her face pale. "Cooper, I can explain–"

"Explain what?" Emily interrupts, her voice sharp. "Mariah, who is this man? And why does he think he's your fiance?"

Mariah's gaze dart between Cooper and me, panic evident in her expression. "I... It's complicated," she stammers.

"Then uncomplicate it," Ewan says, his voice stern. "Now."

Cooper turns to Mariah, confusion and hurt clear in his eyes. "Mariah, what's going on? We had an agreement. I came all the way to help you,a nd now I find out you've replaced me?"

"Replaced?" I can't help but interject. "Is that what you think happened here?"

Cooper rounds on me. "And who exactly are you to be involved in this at all?"

I take a step forward, feeling my temper rise. "I'm the guy who's been here, supporting Mariah, while you're were nowhere to be found."

"Logan, please," Mariah pleads, placing a hand on my arm. Her touch sends a jolt through me but I force myself to focus.

I turn to Cooper. "We went to the airport," I say, trying to fill in the gaps. "We waited but you never showed up."

Cooper explains about losing his phone and wallet, and how Harper found him in Nevada City. As he speaks, I can't help but feel a twinge of jealousy. This is the man Mariah originally chose for this charade. What does that say about me?

"Wait a minute! You're engaged to two men?" Harmony asks, her voice filled with disbelief. "Is this what it is?"

The absurdity of the situation hits me, and I can't help but let out a bitter laugh. "No, she's not," I say, the words tasting like ash in my mouth. "I'm not Mariah's fiance, and neither is Cooper. The whole thing was a charade."

The room falls silent, the weight of my words settling over everyone like a heavy blanket. I can feel their eyes on us, a mix of shock, confusion, and dawning realization.

"A charade?" Harmony's voice is barely above a whisper. "What do you mean?"

Cooper looks between Mariah and me, realization dawning on his face. "You asked someone else to pretend? After our agreement?"

Before me, the warmth and acceptance they'd shown me over the past day fades away, replaced by hurt and betrayal. It's like watching a beautiful painting being washed away by rain, colors bleeding together until the original image is unrecognizable.

"I didn't ask him," Mariah says quickly. "Logan volunteered when you couldn't make it."

"Couldn't make it?" Cooper scoffs. "I lost my phone, Mariah. I did everything I could to get here for you."

I feel a surge of anger. "And where were you when she was panicking about facing her ex? Where were you when she needed someone to lean on?"

"That's not fair," Cooper retorts. "I was doing her a favor-"

"A favor?" I laugh bitterly. "Is that what you call it? Because from where I'm standing, it looks like you were more than happy to play along with this deception."

"Enough!" Ewan's voice cuts through our argument. He turns to Mariah, his expression a mix of disappointment and confusion. "Mariah, explain. Now."

Mariah takes a deep breath, her voice shaky as she begins. "When I heard Elliot and Minerva were coming home for Christmas, I panicked. I... I hired Cooper to pretend to be my fiancé."

A collective gasp fills the room. I watch as the hurt and disappointment settle on her family's faces.

"And Logan?" Emily asks, her voice cold. "Where does he fit into all this?"

Mariah's eyes meet mine for a brief moment before she looks away. "When Cooper couldn't make it, Logan offered to step in. He was just trying to help me."

"Help you lie to us," Ewan says, his voice heavy with disappointment.

I feel the need to defend Mariah, despite everything. "It wasn't like that. We never meant for it to go this far."

Cooper shakes his head. "I can't believe this. I came

all this way, and for what? To be part of some elaborate game?"

"It wasn't a game," Mariah insists, her voice cracking. "I just... I couldn't face everyone alone. Not after everything with Elliot."

The mention of Elliot's name hangs in the air, a reminder of the pain that started all of this. I look at Mariah, seeing the fear and regret in her eyes. Despite everything, I still want to protect her. But as I open my mouth to speak, I realize there's nothing left to say. The truth is out, and with it, any chance of salvaging what Mariah and I might have had.

As the family peppers Mariah and Cooper with questions, I stand there, feeling increasingly out of place. This isn't how I wanted the truth to come out. I wanted us to come clean together, to face this as a team. But now, watching Mariah's face pale with each passing second, I realize how naive that hope was.

"Who the hell volunteers to pretend to be someone's fiancé?" Emily demands.

"A friend," I reply stiffly, fighting to keep my emotions in check.

"He's my mechanic. He and his brother maintain my vans and my SUV," Mariah says coldly, and her tone cuts deep.

Is that all I am to her? Just a mechanic?

Harper jumps to my defense, mentioning the Garrison Bros, but it doesn't matter. The damage is done.

"I can't believe you picked a Garrison Bro over me," Cooper scoffs, and I feel a surge of anger. This isn't a competition, and Mariah isn't a prize to be won.

"So none of it was true?" Ewan looks at me, his voice laced with disappointment. "The things you said about my daughter, it was all made up?"

I clear my throat, my heart pounding. "I meant what I said about how I felt about your daughter," I say, my voice steady despite the turmoil inside me. Because it's true. Every word of affection, every moment of tenderness - it was all real for me.

As Chad's truck approaches, breaking the tense silence that has fallen over the room, I know it's time for me to leave. But there's one last thing I need to do.

"I need to get my bag," I say, my voice sounding hollow even to my own ears. Without waiting for a response, I turn and head up the stairs, acutely aware of the eyes following my every move.

Each step feels heavier than the last as I make my way to the room Mariah and I shared. The room where, just hours ago, I had allowed myself to hope for something more. I pause at the door, my hand on the knob, taking a deep breath before pushing it open.

The room is exactly as we left it this morning, but it feels different now. Colder. Empty. Mariah's suitcase is still open on the floor, clothes spilling out in a colorful array that seems to mock the gray mood that's settled over me.

I move to the corner where I left my backpack, trying

not to let my gaze linger on the bed we shared, on the way her body felt so right against my own, the sound of her sweet giggles and then the feel of her lips against mine...

Some things just aren't meant to be.

With my backpack slung over my shoulder, I take one last look around the room. It's strange how quickly a place can go from feeling like home to feeling like somewhere you don't belong. With a heavy heart, I close the door behind me, the soft click echoing in the quiet hallway.

As I descend the stairs, I half expect – half hope – to see Mariah waiting at the bottom. But the foyer is empty, the family having retreated to the living room, their muffled voices carrying a mix of confusion and hurt.

I clear my throat as I reach the bottom of the stairs, drawing their attention. "I'm sorry for my part in this deception," I say, my voice low and filled with regret. "You've all been incredibly kind to me, and I wish things had turned out differently."

No one speaks as I grab my coat and head for the door. I can't help but glance up the stairs one last time, hoping against hope that Mariah will appear, that she'll ask me to stay, that we can somehow fix this mess we've created. But the staircase remains empty, and I realize it's truly time to let go.

With a final nod to the stunned family, I step out into the cold, the biting wind a welcome distraction from the ache in my chest. As I walk towards Chad's truck, I leave behind the warmth of the house, the promise of belonging, and the dream of what could have been with Mariah.

The door closes behind me with a soft click, a sound of finality. As I climb into Chad's truck, I can't help but wonder if I'll ever see Mariah again, if we'll ever be able to rebuild the friendship we had before all of this. But for now, all I can do is move forward, leaving behind the remnants of a Christmas charade that became all too real.

"You okay, man?" Chad asks as I settle into the passenger seat, concern evident in his voice.

I nod, not trusting myself to speak just yet. As we pull away from the house, I watch it grow smaller in the side mirror, the warm glow of its windows fading into the distance. With it goes the brief, beautiful illusion of the life I might have had – a life with Mariah, a life as part of her family.

But illusions, no matter how sweet, can't last forever. And as the house finally disappears from view, I turn my gaze to the road ahead, ready to face whatever comes next – alone.

CHAPTER 13

Mariah

"What's up?" Forrest asks the moment he opens his front door and I step inside his cabin, not waiting for him to invite me inside.

It's been a few hours since the dramatic confrontation at the main house and although I was glad that the family left me alone, I needed someone to talk to.

It's been a few hours since the dramatic confrontation at the main house and although I was glad that the family left me alone, I needed someone to talk to.

As Bodhi nuzzles his warm nose against my hand, the absence of judgment on my brother's face tells me he hasn't heard the news.

Or maybe he has and he's simply being Forrest.

Unreadable.

But I don't care if he's being his usual quiet and mysterious self or not. I have to tell someone how I'm feeling.

"I made a huge mistake," I blurt out as soon as Forrest shuts the door behind me. "After I learned that Elliot and Minerva were coming home for Christmas, I faked my engagement so I wouldn't show up alone and have everyone feel sorry for me. But the guy I hired got stuck in New York and so, Logan volunteered to be my fiancé and I figured why not? But Cooper just showed up and now, everyone knows what I did and I'm so ashamed. I can't even stay at the house."

"Why not? Did they take out the pitchforks?"

I glare at him as he takes my coat and hangs it behind the door. "That's not funny."

"So that's why Cooper's name was on my present. It's not Logan's first or middle name at all."

"Yes."

"But you and Logan have been seeing each other, right?"

I shake my head as I sit on the couch. "He's just a friend."

His brow furrows. "Really?"

"He was helping me and now we're both in trouble. Harper announced our engagement on social media. Only we're not engaged. We were just pretending to be."

Forrest settles into his armchair across from me. As he leans forward, resting his forearms on his thighs, I can't help but feel lighter after letting it all spill out. Sure, I had that moment with Emily but it's not like this. This feels like a complete—or almost complete— washing away of my sins. But that's because this is

Forrest I'm with, someone I can always trust to have my back, someone who didn't judge too quickly. I should have talked to him first before I launched my hare-brained idea of pretending to be engaged.

But it's too late now.

Still, Forrest is still my brother. He was always my confidante, and his ability to keep secrets is why I've come to talk to him.

Not that I have any more secrets left.

"Please don't tell me I should have known better," I say, sighing. "I already feel terrible as it is."

"Don't worry. I'm not going to say it, not when I'm sure you're already doing an amazing job torturing yourself for it." He gets up from his armchair and heads to the kitchen, opening the refrigerator door. "Care for hot chocolate? I was just about to make some."

"I'd love some." I get up from my chair. "Can I help? I need to do something before I go crazy."

"Guilt can do that to you," he says, grinning when I throw him a dirty look. He cocks his head toward the cupboard. "You can grab the cocoa powder and sugar. Chocolate chips, too."

I smile, the thought of warm chocolate milk reminding me of the days when we were kids, sitting around the table sweetening our sweet chocolate with whatever Mom and Dad would have on the table.

As Bodhi settles back into his dog bed in front of the fire, Forrest lights the stove and pours milk into a large saucepan while I set out whatever toppings I can find, chocolate chips, marshmallows, whipped cream, warm caramel, crushed peppermint canes. We're focused on one thing only and that's making the perfect mug of hot chocolate on a cold winter's day, no matter how terrible said day has turned out to be, at least for me.

Among the siblings, Forrest was always the rock. He was the one we turned to as much as Emily wished she were the strong one. There was always something about his quiet nature that made us gravitate to him—even Emily, for that matter—when times were tough. Or if we just needed someone to listen.

It feels weird seeing him with his hair trimmed and his beard completely gone. He appears ten years younger.

"What made you shave your beard off and cut your hair?" I ask as I set two mugs next to the stove.

"It was time for a change."

"Is it because of Summer?"

He narrows his gaze as he glances at me and shakes his head. "Does everything I do have to revolve around a woman?"

I shrug. "It is a drastic change. One minute you're Mr. Mountain Man and the next, you're Mr. Model."

"Says the woman who says she's engaged but really isn't," he says as he whisks cocoa powder and sugar into the steaming milk.

"Ouch." I pause, handing him the bowl of chocolate chips which he drops into the saucepan. "Point taken."

"I'm sorry, Mariah. That was low," he says. "You had your reasons and they were valid."

I shake my head. "No, they weren't. It was cowardly of me."

"Look, what Elliot and Minerva did was terrible and that's that. No one can expect you to get over that kind of betrayal."

"It's been three years."

"So?" He turns off the flame and pours hot chocolate into the mugs before setting the saucepan back on the stove. "Who says you're supposed to get over it in a year or three years? You got to do you, not follow some guide that some guy who has no idea who you are came up with and preaches as the only way."

"I might as well have. That's why I lied and pretended to be engaged."

"Well, that I don't agree with, but it's done, Mariah. You can't turn back time." He drops two marshmallows into his mug and sprinkles chocolate powder over them. "The only thing you can do now is move on."

I spray whipped cream over my hot chocolate and follow him to the dining table. "How can I face everyone after what I did?"

"You'll have to unless you plan on disappearing on us forever," he says. "Besides, next year, we'll probably be laughing about all this. Or not even remember it."

"What about Logan? I hurt him."

"He's a grown man," Forrest says. "If he agreed to

help you with this... charade, then he knew what he was getting into."

"I didn't expect everyone to like him. *Really like him.* He even fixed Dad's truck and suddenly Mom and Dad wanted a wedding date. They want us to get married right here at the lodge. We didn't expect things to go from zero to six." I sigh and stare at my mug. "I thought he'd just show up, be friendly and then we'd go back to LA and that was that."

"But he does like you," Forrest says. "You know that, right? Or he wouldn't have agreed to help you."

"He's a good friend."

"Is that all he is?"

I pretend not to hear him. "He probably won't have anything to do with me."

Forrest covers my hand with his. "If he's that good of a friend, Mariah, then he'll understand. He may need some time alone, but that's a given. Heck, you might need some time alone yourself. But hopefully, before you do that, spend time with family."

"What about Mom and Dad? And Cooper?" I continue. "The poor guy lost his wallet and still made it here only to end up in the middle of a big mess."

"I suspect he can handle himself, too," Forrest says as we hear a knock on the door. Before he can get up, the door opens and Harper walks in.

"There you are," she says as she stomps her boots on the doormat. "I smell hot chocolate." She takes a deep breath as Cooper walks in behind her.

"Speaking of the devil..." Forrest says, grinning.

"Got any more?" Harper shrugs off her coat and hangs it behind the door. "I'll take it as my fee for the makeover."

"It's on the stove. Should still be warm." Forrest gets up from his chair and walks toward Cooper, extending his hand. "You must be the man of the hour. I'm Forrest."

"Nice to meet you. I'm Cooper." He steals a glance at me before smiling sheepishly. "I'm sorry for making things worse for you, Mariah. I should have taken the snowstorm as a sign that I'd be better off staying where I was."

"Please don't say that. I'm glad you made it and are safe." I stand up and pull up the chair next to me. "Sit. Would you like some hot chocolate?"

"I got it," Harper says as she retrieves two more mugs from the cupboard. "There's enough here for the two of us."

"I'm sorry for running out on you," I say to Cooper as he sits down next to me. "Back at the house."

He shrugs. "No worries. You had other problems to deal with. I hope you and Logan made up."

"He's just a friend," I say, my cheeks burning. "He volunteered to be in your place when you got stuck in New York. We waited for you at the airport."

"You might as well be comfortable." Harper sets a steaming mug of hot chocolate in front of him. "It'll be a few days before you can get your driver's license replaced and I doubt you can fly back to New York without either of them."

"My ID, you mean," Cooper says. "I don't drive."

Harper stares at him. "Do you know how to drive, at least?"

Cooper shakes his head. "Not in Manhattan."

"Lucky you," I mutter. "We have to drive everywhere in LA"

"Is that where you live?" Cooper asks as Harper hands him a mug of hot chocolate along with a bag of marshmallows.

I nod, relieved that the anxiety that had overwhelmed me back at the main house is gone. Or at least, it's not as bad. Cooper also has the kindest blue eyes I've ever seen. It's as if Paul Newman's younger doppelgänger is sitting right next to me.

For the next few minutes, none of us talk as we enjoy our hot chocolate in silence until Harper clears her throat and says my name. My shoulders tense at the reprimand about to come from my younger sister.

"I know you're scheduled to drive back down tomorrow and I want you to know that I'll help Cooper get his passport and ID replaced so he can return home."

"You don't have to–" Cooper begins but Harper holds up her hand.

"You could have stayed behind when your flight got canceled, but you didn't," she says. "Instead, you did all you could to make it here and it's the least we can do for your trouble." She turns to me, a knowing expression on her face "Right, Mariah?"

Before I can reply, there's a brief knock on the door before it opens and Emily and Brad with Jonathan in his arms step inside. As they stomp their boots on the door-mat, Forrest gets up from his chair.

"So this is where you guys are." Emily hangs her coat behind the door. "It got quiet in the main house and I figured we'd probably find you here."

"Care for hot chocolate?" Forrest asks.

"You're having hot cocoa and you guys didn't even call us? How rude." Brad's exaggerated expression of shock has everyone giggling as he lets go of Jonathan who runs straight to Cooper.

"I'm sorry but he just can't get enough of you," Emily says as Jonathan stops in front of Cooper and holds his arms up. "He's not like that. Promise."

"It's no big deal."

"Up! Up!" Cries Jonathan as Cooper glances at Emily and Brad.

"May I?"

"Of course." Brad joins Forrest in front of the stove. "Frees me to have some of my brother-in-law's famous hot chocolate at my leisure. Or however long it takes for him to get bored with his new friend."

"Five minutes," Emily says. "Please let it be at least five minutes."

Cooper laughs as Jonathan climbs on his knee. "It's

no problem. Seriously, he can hang out with me for as long as he wants."

"I want to hang out with him for as long as I want. Can I, please?" Harper whispers in my ear as the door opens and our parents walk in.

"I knew they were all in here, my love," Dad says as he holds the door for Mom.

Harper jumps up from her chair and joins Forrest and Brad in front of the stove as Mom steps inside.

"Do you have enough for two more?" she asks as Bodhi jumps up from his doggy bed and runs to her.

Forrest reaches for a canister from his cupboard. "I have more than enough for everyone. Grab a seat."

"Milk, too?" Emily asks as her brother nods.

"Yup."

Five minutes later, we're all seated around the table enjoying hot chocolate when there's a soft knock on the door. My heart hammers in my chest as everyone but Forrest looks around, wondering if we missed anyone. Then they look at me.

Did Logan come back?

"I'll get it." As Forrest pulls open the door, we stare at Summer standing outside, her eyes widening as she takes us all in.

"I'm sorry I'm late, but..." she pauses when she sees us sitting around the table. "Oh, I'm sorry. I didn't realize you had company. I can come another time–"

"You're exactly the person I was expecting," he says as he takes her coat and hangs it behind the door.

Harper arches her eyebrows. *Did they, like, hook up?* she mouths but I shake my head.

Now's not the time, I mouth back.

While a part of me is disappointed it's not Logan, I'm too caught up in the happy energy permeating throughout the room to worry about him. The last thing I want to do is talk about what happened this morning. No, I don't even want to think about it. It's simply not the time.

As I join in on the conversation about chocolate and how, according to Summer, one can make a delicious tea with cacao shells, my mood shifts.

No more feeling sorry for myself.

No more regrets.

My brother is right.

If Logan is that good a friend—and he is… or was—he'll understand.

What matters right now is that I'm with family.

CHAPTER 14

Logan

LIAM AND I GET BACK FROM MONTEREY ON NEW Year's Eve. We're exhausted but elated from our journey. It felt good to smell the salty air and feel the sun against our faces as we rode up the coast. Heaven knows I needed the break.

While I was pretending to be Mariah's fiancé, Liam and Adriana had decided to do a road trip after Christmas but she couldn't make it after she caught a cold. So when I got back from Northern California on Christmas Day, Liam said I was the lucky guy to accompany him.

He would have stayed to keep an eye on Adriana but after hearing about what happened between me and Mariah, she thought it would be a good idea if the brothers spent some time together.

I definitely had no objection to that. It was something we did all the time although this time, we decided to film the whole thing. Two brothers back on the road again. According to Liam, such trips were in demand with our fans.

As we drive along the freeway heading south on the 405, Liam and I make one more stop before heading home. But first, we hit the supermarket where I buy a bouquet. It's far from the arrangements Mariah normally makes for me every Friday, but I'm not sure about continuing that arrangement. I'm not canceling our standing order just yet, although if I do, I'll do it after the New Year.

Things won't feel as raw then.

I hate how everything changed between us since Christmas. Even Liam can tell but he knows better than to ask for details. He just knows that one moment I was "engaged" on social media and the next, I wasn't. One minute I couldn't stop raving about Mariah and the next, I couldn't stand the sound of her name.

I haven't even returned her calls.

With the GoPro cameras strapped to our helmets and our bikes and the drone equipment we brought with us, there were other things I needed to focus on.

The cemetery is quiet when we arrive. Overlooking the 405 Freeway, you'd think it would be noisy but it isn't. Somehow, you don't hear the sounds of traffic in the distance at all.

For a few months after we buried Mom, Liam and I

would stop by to pay our respects. We'd take the truck which carried the lawn chairs we'd set up in front of her grave and make a picnic out of it. We'd tell her what we were doing and thank her for the graces that came our way.

Visiting her always made Liam and I feel good. But those visits have dwindled through the years. Once a week became once every two weeks until it became a monthly thing although we never missed celebrating her birthday and the holidays. During Holy Week, we'd come here, too, and reminisce about the crazy costumes she used to make for us for Halloween, telling us that her Irish grandparents called it Samhain, believing it was when the veil between the worlds was at its thinnest.

We park our motorcycles at the curb and after I retrieve the bouquet from the saddle bag, we make our way up the hill toward Mom's grave.

Suddenly Liam stops and I almost run right into his back. "Are those flowers from last week?"

I shake my head. "The cemetery staff removes flowers every week, Thursday so there shouldn't be any right now. Maybe Adriana left them."

"She would have told me if she did, considering she's deathly allergic to flowers."

As we draw closer, there's no mistaking the fresh bouquet arranged in the granite lawn vase that's part of Mom's gravestone. It's also an arrangement that Adriana wouldn't know about, not even if Liam told her because he could never name any of the flowers Mom loved, pink Asiatic lilies, purple daisy poms, and alstroemeria interspersed with white waxflowers and purple statice.

Liam gets down on his haunches and runs his finger over one of the lilies' petals. "They're fresh. Maybe from yesterday?"

I shrug. "Maybe her assistant brought it over for her."

"I doubt it," Liam says. "But that was really nice of Mariah to do this when she didn't have to."

My chest tightens as I nod, not saying anything.

Still on his haunches, Liam bends down to smell one of the lilies. "Mom would have been happy to have known her. They'd have gotten along quite well."

I shrug, absently rubbing my boot along the manicured grass. "Probably."

"Alright, that's it." Liam straightens up and faces me. "Can I just get something off my chest right now?"

"Sure."

"You're an idiot, Logan Garrison."

I look at him in disbelief. "Excuse me?"

"You're an idiot," he repeats, shaking his head in disgust.

"So I'm an idiot," I scoff. "Who cares?"

Liam stares at me for a few moments. "I can't believe you're just going to let her go all because she messed up. Once," he says. "So she made a mistake. Big freaking deal. But guess what, bro? Everyone makes mistakes.

Everyone. Even you. And right now, you're making the biggest one."

"Look, we went too far. I should have known better than to–"

"No shit, Sherlock. But it's not as if you wouldn't have wanted to be her fiancé in the first place. Not when you've had the hots for her ever since we first met her." He shoves his finger against my chest before I can protest. "Even when you had some chick on the side, you always dropped everything for Mariah. All it took was a phone call and you were on it. Whatever she wanted, you were there. And don't lie to me and say you weren't." He points to Mom's gravestone. "Not in front of our mother."

"But–"

"You gave her discounts."

"I give many people discounts."

"Not fifty percent off the bill," Liam says. "You even told me to take it out of your pay."

I exhale, my cheeks heating. "Well..."

"I'm just telling you the facts, bro. They're the very facts you don't want to acknowledge. Instead, you run and pretend it's nothing. You even avoid her phone calls," he says as I look at Mom's grave, at the flowers that Mariah must have carefully arranged and then brought over here herself. I can almost see her making sure the flowers looked good in the granite vase, her blond hair falling off her shoulders as she slipped something between the blooms. "Since when did my brother become the biggest idiot I know?"

"Now that's low."

"Yeah, it is."

Suddenly I get down on my haunches and pull out a rolled piece of paper stuck between the blooms.

"What's that?" Liam asks as I stand up and unroll the sheet.

"Looks like a note."

Liam peers over my shoulder. "What does it say?"

The handwriting is neat and familiar. I've seen it before because I've seen Mariah write little thank-you notes for me and the guys every time we do the maintenance on her delivery vans. It's the same handwriting that graces her thank you, birthday, and Christmas cards.

Dear Mrs. Garrison,

Thank you for raising two amazing sons, one of whom I have hurt so much after everything he did for me even when he knew deep down it was wrong to pretend to be someone he wasn't. But no matter how wrong it was to do what we did, I want you to know that he made me so happy. He made me realize I needed to move on from the past that has weighed me down for so long and kept me from *appreciating what (and who) was right in front of me all along. Maybe one day, things will work out again. But for now, I hope you like your flowers. I truly enjoy arranging them for you every week.*

Mariah

As Liam steps back, I'm glad he doesn't insist on reading it. My chest tightens. My mouth feels dry. I roll the note again and slip it back between the flowers, back to the woman I meant it for.

Liam brings his fingers to his lips and rests them lightly on Mom's gravestone, and I'm relieved that he remains silent. Normally, we'd be sharing stories with Mom about our trip, recounting either something foolish Liam did or how I was a total killjoy. These tales usually make us chuckle and shake our heads at how silly they sound in hindsight—something Mom would have pointed out with a certain look when she was alive. Now, all we have is her name etched on a gravestone.

Our mother. Our friend.

Ten minutes later, we say our silent goodbyes to Mom, wishing her a Merry Christmas and a Happy New Year and promising to stop by again soon.

"You hanging out with Adriana?" I ask as we make our way back to our bikes. I'm glad he hasn't pushed the issue about Mariah, and I'm hoping from here on, we won't talk about her.

"Yup, she's got dinner and Netflix planned for us at her mom's place," he replies as he zips up his leather jacket. "You're invited, too, you know."

"Thanks, but I'm good."

He frowns. "You sure? It's New Year's Eve."

I shrug. I can always call the guys from the shop and crash their parties. "Yeah, I'm sure."

Liam snaps on his helmet, leaving the visor up. "Can I say one last thing?"

"No," I mutter even though I know he's going to say it anyway.

"Don't be an idiot," he says. "You've been in love with Mariah since day one and while I have no idea what happened up there, I do know that whatever did happen can't be the end of everything you two have built together through the years. Even as friends." He pauses. "And that's all I've got to say about that. Happy New Year, bro."

I watch Liam ride away, his words echoing in my mind. As the sound of his motorcycle fades into the distance, I find myself turning back towards Mom's grave. The flowers Mariah arranged seem to glow in the fading light of the day, drawing me in.

Before I know it, I'm standing in front of the grave-stone again. I trace my fingers over Mom's name, remembering her warm smile, her infectious laugh. The note from Mariah feels heavy in my pocket, and I pull it out, re-reading her words.

"What would you tell me to do, Mom?" I whisper, my voice barely audible over the rustle of leaves in the evening breeze.

For a moment, I swear I can hear her voice in my head, gentle but firm. 'Follow your heart, honey. But make sure your head's along for the ride too.'

I chuckle softly, shaking my head. Even in my imagination, Mom's practical wisdom shines through.

As the last light of the year fades, casting long shadows across the cemetery, I sit down on the grass next to Mom's grave. The emotions I've been bottling up for days start to surface - the hurt, the confusion, the lingering feelings for Mariah that I can't seem to shake.

"I messed up, Mom," I admit quietly. "I let my pride get in the way. I ran when things got complicated."

A cool breeze brushes against my face, almost like a comforting touch. I close my eyes, imagining Mom sitting beside me, listening patiently as she always did.

"But Mariah messed up too," I continue. "She lied, she put on this whole charade. And yet..." I trail off, looking at the flowers she so carefully arranged. "And yet she's still here, in her own way. Still caring."

As I sit there, pouring out my heart to Mom's silent gravestone, I feel something shift inside me. The anger and hurt that have been clouding my judgment start to dissipate, replaced by a growing clarity.

I stand up, brushing grass off my jeans. "I think I know what I need to do, Mom," I say, resting my hand on top of the gravestone. "It might not be easy, but... I think it's time I stopped running."

With a deep breath, I tuck Mariah's note back into my pocket. I'm not ready to call her yet - some conversations need to happen face to face. But I know where I'll be heading before this year ends.

"Thanks, Mom," I whisper, and I swear I can feel her smile.

CHAPTER 15

Mariah

"YOU SURE YOU DON'T WANT TO COME WITH US tonight?" Cora asks as she gets in the van next to me. "It'll be fun."

"Thanks, but I just want to relax," I reply, glancing at the side mirror to make sure two of my other employees got in the second van that carried the rest of the arrangements for the event. "This event has tired me out and all I want is to curl up on my couch and watch all the NYE celebrations streaming on TV."

"Where's the fun in that?"

I chuckle. "You'd be surprised at how much fun doing nothing can be."

And that's really all I've been doing the moment I get home. With the biggest event of the year done and dusted, I'm ready to do absolutely nothing tonight. The wedding of the century, as the press dubbed the wedding, goes on tonight but by then, I'll be sitting on my couch with my feet up doing nothing. I've also been up since three in the morning supervising all the arrangements for the event, not to mention working nonstop since I got back from my parents' house.

I sigh. At least, no one mentioned Logan after we spent the evening at Forrest's cabin. It was cramped with everyone there plus poor Autumn whom we probably overwhelmed two nights in a row, but it was just what I needed to get over the stunt I tried to pull on my family.

It'll probably be one of those stories everyone avoids to talk about in the coming years and if so, I'll be relieved.

At least, Cooper's on his way to getting his ID and credit cards replaced, thanks to Harper who dropped everything from her calendar to help him. She even convinced our parents to put him in one of the cabins. After everything he'd been through, we couldn't just throw him out of the lodge—thanks to yours truly.

As for Logan, I haven't heard from him since he left the Soraya with his friend Chad. And maybe it's for the best.

I've tried not to check his social media account but in the end, I couldn't stop myself. A peek at the social media accounts Logan shares with his brother revealed that he and Liam were riding their bikes up to Monterey.

Actually, it was more than just a peek.

He seemed happy in the pictures with the ocean behind him. Some photos were taken from a drone high above, offering majestic views of the coast. If he's trying to move on, he's doing it in style and I can't blame him. I just wish I could talk to him one last time.

But if I can't—if he'd rather not talk to me again—that's okay, too.

Life goes on.

When the last of my employees clock out at six, I'm left alone in the shop for the first time since I walked in at three in the morning. I should be out partying—after all, it's New Year's Eve—but after being on my feet for fifteen hours straight, all I want to do is go home, take a shower, and greet the new year in my dreams.

At least, even if my love life is in shambles and is nonexistent, I just closed the year with a bang. The NYE-themed wedding was the biggest event my employees and I have ever handled. I even ran out of business cards to hand out. The other vendors setting up for the event were impressed and curious about my little flower shop. Even a network crew covering the wedding submitted a standing order for Always on a Tuesday Flowers to provide flowers for their offices and if I wasn't exhausted right now, I'd probably stay longer so I can work on flower choices.

After all, I need to stay busy so I don't think about Logan.

The knock on the front door snaps me back to the present and I glance at the clock on the wall, knowing that whoever it is and whatever they need, the shop will remain closed. No exceptions. But I peek anyway and my heart skips a beat when the man outside the front door smiles sheepishly.

Who am I kidding?

Logan Garrison will always be an exception.

I unlock the front door and let him in. He's wearing black jeans and a dark t-shirt under a denim shirt, looking gorgeous as ever.

"I saw the light and thought I'd stop by, if that's okay."

"Sure." I step aside. "Come in."

As he brushes past me, I detect the scent of a familiar blend and look at him quizzically.

Spruce and rosewood.

"Is that from my mom?" I ask as I close the door behind me.

He nods. "She gave me soaps and a bottle of insect repellent for Christmas. All organic, of course, and the repellent worked during our ride to Monterey. Even Liam wants one now."

"Yup, that's Mom all right." I lean against the door as I face him, not quite knowing what to do next except that I don't want him to leave right away. "By the way, Happy New Year."

"Happy New Year, Mariah," he says, taking a deep breath. "I've missed you."

I catch my breath. "I've... I've missed you, too."

"I'm sorry about the way things went down between

us," he says. "I'm sorry for leaving you up there the way I did. I should have stood by you until the end, as your friend, at least. Instead, I left and that was wrong."

My throat tightens. "You had every reason to leave, Logan. You didn't want to pretend anymore and you were right. I wouldn't have stood by me either, not after everything fell apart the way it did and Cooper arriving–"

"I just wanted us to be real, Mariah, you and me, and what we had going," he says. "I wanted it all to be real. You, your family, and the love you all shared. I wanted it all even when I knew what we had was pretend."

I swallow, my mouth suddenly feeling dry. "Not all of it."

"It definitely wasn't for me. But you already know that."

Like him, I'd wished everything to be real, but I panicked the moment Cooper showed up and I became the girl who didn't want people to think she hadn't moved on from being betrayed.

"What happened to the ring?" he asks and I glance down at my hands, my fingers bare.

"It's in my jewelry box," I reply. "It wasn't real... even if it looked nice."

Logan brings my hand to his lips. "Would you like us to be real, Mariah? Because I do."

As I gaze at him, I see the pain in his eyes mingled with a yearning I remember when we were at the Cercis, just before things fell apart. That was when he bared everything to me, telling me how he really felt. But instead of being strong, I scuttled back into the safety of my past, putting up the wounds I used as armor.

But I can't do that anymore. I'm done living in the past.

"Yes," I whisper, the rest of my answer translated into the kiss that comes when Logan's lips meet mine, my entire being breathing him in like he's the air I need to survive. My arms circle his neck, the taste of his lips reminding me of the laughter we shared as we sat in front of the Christmas tree with my family just a few days ago, the smell of pine and the feel of snow beneath our boots as we took that first walk around the Soraya... and then that practice kiss that was never a practice kiss at all, not for us.

Logan pulls away and studies my face, his thumb stroking my cheek. "I saw the flowers you left at my mother's grave," he murmurs. "That was really nice of you."

"When you didn't show up, I figured you were probably still out of town," I say. "I couldn't tell from the social media pictures."

He grins. "You looked."

I bite my lip. "I tried not to."

"I'm glad you did, but you're right. We were making our way back down."

"And her grave would have been without flowers for the week." I pause. "I hope you don't mind me doing that. The thought of you finding another florist occurred to me but when I saw that her grave was empty–"

"I'd never consider another florist, Mariah, but thank you for thinking about her." When I don't say anything, Logan continues. "I read your note. I know it wasn't for me and I'm sorry."

"I hope that was okay."

"You two would have gotten along well. Even Liam said so," he says.

"Logan, I owe you an apology, too."

"What for?"

"I'm sorry for telling everyone you were just my mechanic. I didn't even have the decency to call you my friend and I am so sorry. I was a coward." I see his jaw clench but he doesn't reply. "You were never just a mechanic to me, Logan. You were always someone special, but I was just too scared to open myself up to falling in love again. Thank goodness, there was always a reason for me to bring them in and see you. Delivery vans do need regular maintenance."

"That's why they call it a maintenance schedule," he says, stroking my cheek with the back of his fingers. "I don't even care if you like pineapple on your pizza, Mariah. I just might give it another try. I simply don't want to lose you again, or ever, for that matter."

As Logan continues to stroke my cheek with his thumb, his fingers grazing the skin behind my ear, I can feel that familiar tingle running down my body and the butterflies in my belly fluttering again. Somewhere in the neighborhood, someone is setting off fireworks.

"So what should we do now?" I ask. "My plans were pretty boring. Go home, take a shower, and greet the new year in my PJs."

A mischievous smile graces his handsome face and he pretends to think for a moment.

"How about celebrating New Year's Eve with me? We can work out the details later."

"Sounds like a plan," I say, chuckling. "Anything else?"

"This." Our lips connect then and I feel myself melting against him. His kiss starts soft at first before becoming hard, his teeth nibbling my lower lip. It's possessive and rough, almost turning my knees into putty.

"Just this?" I ask, breathless.

"There is more we can do."

"I'd like that," I murmur as he kisses me again, his kiss deepening with every passing second.

Suddenly Logan drags his mouth from my lips. "Let's get out of here before I end up doing more right on your counter."

I nip playfully at his lower lip. "I do have a larger-than-twin-size bed in my apartment."

"That's good to know."

I frown. "There is one problem, though."

He frowns. "What?"

"I'm starving. And the last thing I want to do is greet

the new year with an empty stomach."

Two hours later, we find ourselves sitting on the floor in front of my fireplace as the Times Square NYE special airs on TV. I've taken a quick shower and we're drinking champagne from plastic flutes and eating pizza we picked up on the way home. Pizza is half pepperoni and the other half pineapple and ham. Logan even braved a taste, doing his best not to make the funniest faces. Our little celebratory meal is nothing like the wedding I just oversaw but I'll take this moment over anything else. At least, this time there is no charade.

As everyone is waiting for the crystal ball to descend over Times Square on a rainy night (even though it's already descended in New York City and we're simply watching the delayed telecast), Logan turns away from the TV and gazes at me.

His fingers trace the outline of my cheekbone, my jawline, my lips. I close my eyes, savoring every sensation as my hands do some tracing of their own, the hard contours of his bicep up to his shoulder and down his chest, and lower still to his six-pack abs.

I don't know what's going to happen tomorrow but I know what I want to happen tonight. This time, we're not pretending.

"Kiss me, Logan," I whisper as he groans, his fingers diving into my hair, pulling me closer. Our mouths meet again, hard and demanding, our tongues tasting of champagne.

"Do you know how long I've waited for this moment, Mariah?" he asks when I pull away to catch my breath.

"How long?"

"Since you started coming to the shop with your vans," he replies, chuckling. "Only then, I told myself to keep everything business."

"Funny. That's me, too, but I always thought you had a girlfriend, like your brother."

Logan thinks for a few moments, his expression serious. Then he shrugs, "Nah, I'm just shy."

I laugh. "No, you're not."

"You're right. I'm not," he says, grinning as I pull him to me.

"Just kiss me, Logan. No more talking."

He chuckles as he lowers his face to mine. "Yes, Ma'am."

He lowers his mouth to mine and I feel my body sigh. As his kiss deepens, Logan's hands roam over my body, pulling me ever closer. I can feel his hard muscles beneath his shirt as I run my fingers through his hair.

The taste of him is intoxicating, my lips drawn to his like a magnet. The heat between us grows with each passing second. We're making up for lost time. So much time.

As we part for a moment to catch our breath, I see the hunger in the eyes. It's the same hunger that burns deep inside me, the one I've pushed away for so long. But not anymore. I know that tonight, I'm his and he's mine, all mine. There's no more denying the connection between us, our friendship still there but this time there's also this.

We're two halves of the same whole, drawn together

The kiss deepens as Logan's hands roam over my body, pulling me ever closer. I feel his hard muscles beneath his shirt as my hands run through his hair. The taste of him is intoxicating, my lips drawn to his like a magnet. The heat between us grows with each passing moment, my mind a blur of desire and passion. His touch sets me on fire, and I want nothing more than to give in to him completely.

Every kiss, every touch feels like electricity sparking between us, igniting a fire that we can no longer ignore.

As we part for a moment to catch our breath, I can see the hunger in his eyes, the same hunger that burns deep within me. I know that I'm his, and he's mine, and there's no denying the connection between us. We're two halves of the same whole, drawn together by an irresistible force.

Suddenly fireworks explode in the distance and on the TV screen, the countdown begins.

Ten...nine...eight...

"It's almost the New Year," I say as Logan pulls away to look at the TV screen.

Six...five...four...

I kiss the tip of his nose. "Happy New Year, Mr. Garrison."

Two...one.

"Happy New Year, Miss Peters." He kisses me on the lips, grinning. "Come here."

As Logan wraps his arms around me, there's nothing else I want to do but greet the New Year like this, moving on together as the world turns on a new leaf, a new year.

A new beginning, this time, for us.

Epilogue

MARIAH

Two months later, the Soraya Lodge looms before us, its timber frame construction stark against the freshly fallen snow. The parking lot is filled with cars, their respective owners likely checking in for a long weekend of skiing or snowboarding. Through the window, a sign at the front desk read "No Vacancy".

It's times like these when Mom and Dad enjoy the influx of visitors to the lodge, regaling them with stories about the area or in Mom's case, about the efficacy of certain crystals depending on their current need.

Love? Try rose quartz to heal old love wounds first and then follow it with malachite or amazonite.

Need clarity? Why not try amethyst or citrine?

I probably have enough rose quartz to last me a lifetime as well as a wire-wrapped malachite pendant that Mom sent me as soon as she heard that Logan and I were seeing each other a month after we left the Soraya.

"For real this time?" she'd asked over the phone, suspicion evident in her voice.

"Yes," I reply, feeling no guilt this time. I left that behind when I asked for everyone's forgiveness. "I promise I won't lie to you ever again about that or anything else for that matter. We've been officially dating since New Year's Eve."

That's when she sent me the malachite pendant the following week and for Logan, a bracelet made of hematite and malachite beads. And he's worn it ever since he received it, removing it only when he's working with engines so it doesn't get dirty.

We're actually on a date, four straight days of doing nothing but relaxing. It's one of the things Logan has wanted to do since we officially started dating—to come back up here so we can face my parents and show them that this time, it's real.

No more lies, no more charades.

No work, either. No phone calls from the shop for the next four days, not even to check the sales numbers. That will be Harper's job, now that she's part of the flower shop, too.

Still, there's no denying how nervous I am to see my parents again, not after what happened and how disappointed they were when they learned the truth about my engagement. But what's done is done. What matters most is what's happened since then and I couldn't be happier. While our businesses have both exploded ever since the New Year and getting together has often been a challenge, our return to the lodge marks a chance for a do-over. We even get our very own cabin.

Except for Harper who's holding down the fort in L.A., everyone else has come down for a mini reunion of sorts. They all greet us the moment we arrive at the house. Over coffee and freshly baked cookies, we talk about what everyone's been up to, from Emily and Brad who are trying for a second baby to Forrest who's busy leading snowshoe hikes with his new girlfriend.

Summer, the woman who ended up at the lodge alone on Christmas Eve.

Afterward, the men head to the garage to talk shop while Mom and Emily pull me aside to quiz me about the New Year's Eve wedding that put my small flower shop on the map after the bride raved about it to a major lifestyle magazine. That's why Harper is manning the fort while I'm gone because business ballooned, and I couldn't handle everything by myself anymore. It helps that she's not exactly alone either. Cooper moved down to L.A.to join her.

"What are your plans now that everything's real?" Emily asks after all the business questions have been answered. "Everything is real this time, right?"

"Of course, it's real, Em. But there's no rush. Right now, we're dating like two normal people would," I reply. "We've been officially dating for two months."

"When's the big date?" Emily asks. "It's not like you guys didn't know each other for years before you officially started dating."

"We're taking things one day at a time," I say. With business at the shop booming and the Garrison Bros scheduled to go on sponsored road trips throughout the coast for their YouTube channel, time spent together has been sparse. So we've got nothing planned for the next four days. Just us and the family.

"Whatever you're thinking, Em, it's too soon for that," I say.

"But you love him, don't you? You two were perfect for each other from day one."

"Nothing is ever too soon," Mom says, grinning. "After all, you guys were already kinda engaged during the holidays."

I roll my eyes. "Mom, that was different. We were pretending."

She looks at me with a faint smile, her eyes glinting mischievously. "Were you, really?"

"Mom, one day it'll happen."

She clasps my hands. "You know what my dream is? That all my daughters get married right here on the same day. That would be a sight, wouldn't it?" She turns to Emily, sighing. "You and Brad, too. A renewal of vows."

This time, Emily's the one who rolls her eyes. "Oh, Mom. It's too soon for that."

Mom winks. "Is it?" She pauses, laughing. "No matter. I'm determined to plant the seed."

The sound of footsteps on the deck signals the return of the men from the garage and an end to any more questions about Logan and me. I jump up from the couch, joining Logan at the door.

"Hey, you," he says, kissing me fully on the lips in front of everyone. "Would you like to take a walk with me before it gets dark?"

I nod. "Definitely. Let me grab my coat."

We hike along one of the easy trails around the lodge, enjoying our time together and not caring who sees us. With guests coming and going, enjoying all the activities Auburn Springs offers, we take advantage of the anonymity and privacy. We even have a playful snowball fight which Logan starts as we make it back to our cabin. But I get him good with one snowball hitting him smack in the face. He laughs, tackling me to the ground before kissing me, his lips cold against mine.

I giggle. "Your lips are cold."

"So are yours. But it'll warm up soon enough," he says as he gets to his feet and helps me up. "Come on, I want to check something out."

"What?"

"Where it all started."

"Where what started?" I frown, not knowing what he means but the moment I see where we're headed, it makes sense. The little bridge where we had our first kiss.

"This is where it officially started," he says when we get to the middle of the bridge and look around us. I can see the main house. I can even see my parents standing by the window. Emily is standing on the deck.

"I've been waiting for this moment for a while now," Logan continues as I turn to look at him.

"What moment?"

"Kissing you again... for real this time."

"But we've been kissing for real since the New Year. Actually, we've been doing more than just kissing," I say, laughing but Logan looks serious.

"You know what I mean, Mariah."

I hold my breath as he cups my face in his hands. There's that same intensity in his eyes that I love, the one that tells me that underneath the happy-go-lucky persona that people know, there's a man who's serious about life, especially when it comes to love and family. I close my eyes as Logan lowers his face toward mine, the feel of his lips warm and soft. My arms wrap around his neck as his kiss deepens, heat racing through my body. I can never get enough of Logan, not his eyes and that smile that always makes every moment better, nor those arms that know when to hold me and keep me safe. Definitely not his heart that never seems to fear being true.

"I love you, Mariah."

"I love you, too, Logan," I say, wanting to ask him what's going on. But before I can, Logan gets down on one knee in front of me and pulls out a small box from his coat pocket.

I bring my hand to my mouth, my mind going a mile a minute as I look around us. Is it true? No, can't be. Is he really doing it... right here while my parents and sister are standing by the window watching us?

"Will you marry me, Mariah Peters? For real this time?"

But even with the rush of questions, my rational brain going a mile a minute, my heart knows the answer. It always did and there is no hesitation.

"Yes, Logan Garrison. I will marry you," I reply, pulling him up to his feet and kissing him as my parents join Emily and Brad on the deck, all of them cheering happily. "For real this time."

Thank you so much for reading! I hope you enjoyed Mariah and Logan's story!

Read Forrest's story in The Reluctant Fiancee from geni.us/reluctantfiancee

If you'd like to be among the first to know what I'm publishing next, sign up for my newsletter at lizduranobooks.com/subscribe.

When tech executive Summer Avila cancels her wedding to her Silicon Valley business partner, she escapes to a forgotten cabin reservation in the snowy mountains for Christmas Eve. There she meets Forrest Peters, a rugged lodge manager whose world of family traditions and mountain solitude challenges everything about her tech-driven life.

As their connection deepens, Summer faces a crisis at her company that forces her to choose: return to her carefully controlled corporate world, or risk everything for love in the wilderness. But can Forrest, still guarding his heart from past wounds, take a chance on someone from such a different world?

Liz's start in storytelling got its rocky start in 8th grade when the "play" she was writing landed her in the principal's office for being a bit on the NSFW side. She has since majored in Journalism and Advertising only to realize once again that she'd rather write stories about people falling in love and getting into trouble, though not necessarily in that order.

When she's not writing about her muses, Liz loves spending time with her family and drinking way too much coffee. She lives in a tiny century-old house a few blocks from the beach with her family, a Chihuahua, and way too many books.

You can follow Liz's book adventures by visiting lizduranobooks.com or follow her on Facebook at @lizduranobooks.